# WE WERE THERE
## ON THE
# *NAUTILUS*

*Every instrument was under constant observation*

# WE WERE THERE
# ON THE
# NAUTILUS

By *ROBERT N. WEBB*

*Historical Consultant:* CAPTAIN WILLIAM R. ANDERSON, U.S.N.

*Illustrated by* FRANK VAUGHN

GROSSET & DUNLAP   *Publishers*

NEW YORK

PRINTED IN THE UNITED STATES OF AMERICA

*We Were There on the Nautilus*

# Contents

# Contents

# Illustrations

# ILLUSTRATIONS

*WE WERE THERE*
ON THE
*NAUTILUS*

# CHAPTER ONE

## *Caught Under Water*

---

H OW about here?"

"Suits me. You figure we're what—two hundred—three hundred feet from shore?"

"More like two hundred, I'd say."

"Okay. Get your breath. When you're ready, say the word."

The two boys, Tim Borden and Steve Kranik, were treading water off the west bank of the Thames River in New London, Connecticut. They had swum slowly out toward the river's channel, getting ready for the race that always ended their daily swim.

"Hey, Cathy!" Tim shouted at the girl sitting on the riverbank. "We're ready. You start us!"

"All right, Timmy. Here you go. Ready! Get set! GO!"

The boys churned the water as they headed for shore. Tim's long arms stretched out in smooth, graceful strokes. His friend and rival, Steve, chopped at the water with short, powerful strokes. They were head and head for the first fifty feet. At the halfway mark, Tim pulled slightly ahead. His feet thrashed at the water. Steve increased his stroke and pulled even. Twenty-five feet to go. Again Tim took the lead. Steve called on every ounce of his strength. The water churned and boiled. Bubbles of foam marked the lanes made by the racers.

The boys' hands touched bottom at the same time. Both flipped over on their back immediately. Each raised his right hand to signal the end of the race. First hand up was the winner.

After a few moments to catch their breath, the boys crawled out of the water and threw themselves on the sandy bank, exhausted. Their chests rose and fell, and they sucked in welcome air.

"Who won? Me?" Tim asked Cathy.

"Well—I think you got your hand up first," Cathy said. "But it looked to me as if Steve was actually ahead of you. Not much, though."

"So if my hand was up first, I'm the winner." Tim spoke the words between gasps for breath.

"Not much you are," his friend Steve grunted. "Cathy says I was ahead of you. So I win."

The boys rose to a half-sitting, half-reclining position, resting on their elbows. They looked at Cathy with big question marks in their eyes.

"All right . . . I'll call it a tie."

"Jeepers!"

"Hunh!"

The boys let themselves fall back to the ground.

Cathy laughed at the disgusted expression which came over the boys' faces. Cathy Kranik was a pretty girl, blond, not too tall, and just a little bit plump. She had a red bud for a mouth. When she laughed, she showed strong, even white teeth. Cathy was almost sixteen. When people—especially her brother Steve—reminded her that she was still only fifteen, she didn't like it one little bit. Cathy could hardly wait to be sixteen so she could say, "I'm going on seventeen."

"How long are you two going to lie there?" she asked the boys.

"Jeepers, sis. Let us have a breather. That was a hard race. Why don't you take another swim or something?"

"All right. Are you going in again?"

"Not me," Tim said. "I've had enough."

Cathy took her brother's face mask and snorkel and waded out into the river. She adjusted the mask to her face and placed the snorkel, a short, plastic breathing tube, to her mouth. Face down, she paddled out, looking down at the river bottom.

Tim sat up. He leaned forward, hands forming a prop for his face, his elbows on his thighs. He stared across the river at Groton.

"That's where we'll be in about a year," he said.

"Where will we be in a year?" Steve asked, sitting up.

"Over there. At the sub base. Where did you think I meant?"

"Oh," Steve replied somewhat sheepishly. "I didn't see where you were looking."

The two boys looked across the river. They could see the lean gray navy ships—sub tenders, submarine rescue ships. Navy tug boats plied up and down the river, scurrying on errands like fat, squat hens.

"Hey! Look! That's a sub coming out!"

They watched the low-lying boat make its way out to midstream. It looked like a tremendously long whale. Its "sail," or conning tower, rode twelve feet above the sub's deck, looking like a fat smokestack floating by itself downstream. The sub's deck rode only a few feet above the water.

"Can you tell which one she is?" Steve asked.

"Could it be the *Nautilus?*"

"Or the *Sea Wolf,*" maybe.

"No, the *Sea Wolf's* at sea. With the fleet. I saw that the other day in the paper. She's out on maneuvers."

"Then it's got to be the *Nautilus,*" Steve said.

"And one of these days, you and I are going to be part of her crew," Tim said firmly.

"Just like that, huh?" Steve said, snapping his fingers. Tim gave him a look but said nothing.

They watched as the *Nautilus* moved slowly

down the Thames River heading for Block Island Sound and the open sea.

Tim and Steve had been the closest of friends from the first day they entered New London High School as freshmen.

Tim Borden had been born and brought up in New London. All his life he had watched the United States Navy's underseas arm, the boats of the Submarine Service, put out to sea, return from maneuvers, go into drydock, be refitted, then rejoin the Atlantic Fleet for maneuvers or patrol duty.

For as long as he could remember, he had always given the same answer when an uncle or a neighbor would ask, "What are you going to be when you grow up, Tim?"

"A submariner," Tim always answered proudly.

Steve Kranik and his family had moved to New London from Kansas City five years before. Steve's father worked for the Electric Boat Division of the General Dynamics Corporation in Groton. Electric Boat had built the *Nautilus,* the first atomic-powered submarine. From him, both boys had learned much about the famous submarine.

Steve was just as anxious to serve on the *Nautilus* as Tim was.

[ *8* ]

The boys had been absolutely quiet as they followed the *Nautilus'* course until her sail was a black dot on the horizon.

"Gee, Tim, I'll tell you something. I never thought I'd make it," Steve said, breaking the silence.

"Make what? Oh, you mean joining the Navy," Tim answered. "You didn't! Why not?"

"All those tests and examinations. I knew you'd make it all right. But me—I don't learn as fast as you do." Steve said.

"What are you worried about? You made it, didn't you?" Tim replied.

It was near the end of June, 1957. School days were behind the boys. They had graduated from New London High School two weeks before. One week before their graduation, just after dinner, the telephone had rung in the Kranik home. It was Tim calling Steve.

"Hey, Steve! I just asked my dad. He said it was all right!" There was so much excitement in Tim's voice that only Steve would have been able to understand what his friend was talking about.

"How 'bout you? Did you ask yet?"

"Dad's not home yet. He's working the late shift."

"I thought you were going to ask him before he went to work." Tim's voice sounded disappointed.

"I know. I was going to, but—gee, Tim, I was just about to and then—"

"Well, you better ask him tonight. Then call me. Right away. No matter what he says."

"Okay, Tim. Be seeing you."

The day had been Steve's birthday. He was seventeen, a few weeks younger than Tim. The boys had solemnly pledged to one another that on the day Steve became seventeen, they would ask their parents for permission to join the Navy.

The Navy takes volunteers when a boy reaches the age of seventeen, if they have their parents' consent. Tim and Steve wanted that permission more than they wanted anything else. If they enlisted at seventeen, they could choose the branch of the Navy they wanted to serve in—and there was no doubt in Tim's and Steve's minds. For them, it was the Submarine Service or nothing.

That was why it had been so important to get their parents' permission to enlist.

The past three weeks had been busy ones for the boys. It all seemed to them as if it had happened just yesterday. There had been so much to do since that first day, when Tim and Steve had walked down Masonic Street to the Navy Recruiting Office in the Post Office building. Tim led the way, pretending a confidence he was far from feeling. Steve had held back slightly. But he didn't hesitate when Tim walked boldly into the small office and spoke to the Chief Petty Officer in charge of recruiting in the New London area.

"Sir, we want to join the Navy," Tim had said.

Half an hour later, after a friendly talk with Chief Vormack, the boys were taking an examination. "Gosh, sir, I thought we were all through with tests and examinations when we got out of high school," Steve said shyly.

Chief Vormack laughed. "You don't know it, but your testing periods are just starting."

And they were. That first test, taken half an hour after the boys entered the Recruiting Office, hadn't been too hard. It took about an hour.

"You both did fine," the chief told them. "Now tomorrow, you get your big tests. They're held at AFES—that's the Armed Forces Examination Station in Springfield, Massachusetts. You'll have to be here bright and early. Bus leaves for Springfield at eight o'clock. You'll get through there about three in the afternoon. The bus will bring you back to this office."

*"Sir, we want to join the Navy."*

The next day's examinations had been longer and tougher. The extent of their general knowledge had been tested in mathematics, science, word meanings, and perception by identifying variously shaped pieces of wood. After these tests came the physical exam. Both boys breezed through this one. Steve had played a hard, crashing fullback at New London High. Tim had ranged far and wide on the football field as a fast, surehanded end.

When the bus brought them back to the Recruiting Office in New London, Chief Vormack was awaiting them.

"Congratulations, boys. You both made it."

"You mean you know already?" The boys were surprised. They had thought it would take much longer to find out if they had passed.

"Oh, sure. They score those tests as soon as you finish them, then they call us. Looks like you're in, boys."

In all New London, no two boys were happier than Tim Borden and Steve Kranik.

Within the next week, Chief Vormack had visited both the Borden and Kranik homes. He had met the boys' parents and explained to them what the Navy could mean to the boys' future.

Mr. Kranik and Mr. Borden signed the official Navy form authorizing their sons to enlist at the age of seventeen.

"Now when do you want to go in? Officially, I mean?" the chief had asked.

Tim and Steve exchanged glances.

"You'll find out you have more to do than you think," the chief said. "Why don't you make it about three weeks from now? Say July fifth. That'll let you spend the Fourth of July holiday at home. Then, it's off you go."

That was the date settled upon. July 5, 1957.

The time had melted away as the boys enjoyed their few short weeks at home. Cathy had kept them busy with sports and parties, insisting each time, "You won't *be* here very much longer."

"Three days to go, Steve," Tim said now, tossing a shell toward the water from the sandy bank where they were sitting.

"Hey, you read my mind," Steve laughed. "I was just thinking the same thing. Three more days, and we'll be in the Navy— Say, we'd better head for home. Supper's not too far off."

Steve stood up.

"Cathy! Hey, Cathy, come on. Time we got started for home."

"In a minute," Cathy called back. "I just saw something on the bottom. I want to find out what it is."

"All right. But hurry."

Tim was standing beside Steve. They watched Cathy go under the surface, her legs and feet finally following the rest of her body down.

"Let's get our gear together."

The boys gathered up the other face mask and snorkels and wrapped them in their towels.

"Hey, Cathy! Cathy!" Steve stood at the edge of the river. Tim joined him.

"She's been down there some time, hasn't she?" Tim said worriedly. "More'n just a few minutes."

"Yeah. What's that?" Steve exclaimed, pointing.

On the surface, directly over the spot where they had seen Cathy submerge, they saw bubbles breaking the surface. The plastic snorkel swirled slowly in the current.

"She must be stuck! Or caught!"

The boys plunged into the river and raced to the spot, leaving a boiling wake behind them.

# CHAPTER TWO

## *Off to Boot Camp*

---

IN SECONDS, the boys were over the spot where Cathy had last been seen. They dived like porpoises toward the bottom. Their eyes strained; their heads pivoted back and forth as they searched the depths for a glimpse of Cathy's white swimming suit.

Tim spotted the struggling girl first. His eyes caught a swirling flash of white as Cathy fought to free herself. With a powerful leg thrust Tim plunged to her side. He grasped her around the waist and kicked, trying to bring the girl and himself to the surface. As he kicked and thrashed, Steve's body shot past him.

Searching with frantic hands, Steve located the trouble. One sharp fluke of a heavy, rusty anchor

[ *16* ]

had become caught in the ruffled red skirt of Cathy's swim suit. Fighting to hold his breath, Steve tore at the material. He ripped open the hole in the cloth until it was large enough for him to yank out the fluke.

The three shot to the surface, breaking the water with open mouths, gasping for needed breath. For a few moments, they could do no more than keep their heads above water, as fresh air flowed back into their lungs. Tim kept one hand in the small of Cathy's back, supporting her head above water.

Tim and Steve started making their way slowly toward shore, towing Cathy on her back between them. As they reached shallow water, Cathy shook herself free, turned over and made the last few feet on her own. She half-stumbled onto the beach and stretched out to rest.

The boys looked at her carefully, worriedly. They could see that she was all right, but it had been a close squeak. A few more seconds and their gay swimming party might have become a tragedy.

Both wanted to know more about what had happened, but held back their questions until Cathy felt stronger. After several moments, the girl raised herself to a sitting position. Her eyes went from her brother's face to Tim's, then swung back.

"You—you saved my life," she said in a weak voice. "Thanks. Thank you both." Then tears came into her eyes, and she brought her hands to her face to hide them.

The boys, embarrassed, sat silent, their heads lowered, until Cathy's sobbing stopped.

"What happened, sis?" Steve asked in a quiet voice.

Cathy bit her lower lip and closed her eyes briefly before answering.

"I was floating, face down, using the snorkel. I could just make out the outlines of that anchor, lying on the bottom in a patch of white sand."

"That's when you first called to us," Tim said.

"Yes. I thought it would be fun to bring that anchor up. Might be an old one, maybe valuable. Perhaps off an old, old boat. So I dived down for it."

She paused. "I didn't have any idea it would be so heavy. I raised it from the sand and held it by its flukes. Then I saw it was too heavy for me to bring to the surface. My breath was getting short, too. So I let go of it and started to spring up to the surface."

"And instead of falling away from you, the anchor fell against you," Tim said.

"I guess that must have been what happened, Tim. The point of one of the flukes got caught in the skirt of my swimming suit, and I couldn't get it out. I was anchored." Cathy tried a faint smile at her last remark.

Steve frowned.

"Oh, I know it wasn't funny," Cathy hastened to add. "And if you two hadn't been here—"

"Don't you ever try anything like that again, Cathy," Steve said seriously. "Especially without one of us being with you."

"And you'll both be gone in just three more days," Cathy said mournfully.

Tim and Steve nodded their heads and stood up. "Feel like we can start for home now, Cathy?" Tim asked.

"Oh, sure. I feel fine now. Don't tell Mama and Papa about this afternoon, please?"

"Guess there's no sense in worrying them," Steve agreed. "But you've got to promise never to try anything like that again."

"I promise," Cathy said soberly.

The three gathered up their swim gear and headed for home.

[ *19* ]

The clock over the stove in the Kranik kitchen showed exactly seven o'clock. Breakfast dishes were still on the table, forgotten in the bustle of activity. Mrs. Kranik, Steve and Cathy's mother, a short, plump woman wearing a red-and-blue apron, moved constantly from the kitchen to the living room and back.

As she went from one room to the other, she kept reading to herself, more than to her son, from an official U. S. Navy form called APPLICANT'S ORDERS.

"Now you're sure you have everything they told you to take, Stephen?"

"Yes, Mama," Steve replied.

Paying no attention to her son's answer, Mrs. Kranik bustled back into the living room to inspect for the fiftieth time Steve's open suitcase, which was resting on a chair.

". . . and you're sure you haven't got any chewing gum in there . . ."

"No, Mama."

". . . or shoe polish, or anything that's glass, like a framed picture?"

"No, Mama, I haven't taken any of the things the Navy said I mustn't take."

The form Mrs. Kranik was reading—she had

read it so often she knew it by heart—was the official list of things for a recruit TO TAKE and NOT TO TAKE.

Cathy was fluttering about, too. The only quiet members of the Kranik family on this important morning were Steve's father, and Steve's younger brother and sister, Billy and Mary. They sat on chairs in the kitchen munching bread and jam.

The telephone rang. Cathy leaped for it.

"Yes, yes. This is Cathy." She lowered her voice and turned her back to the others in the room, to muffle the words she was speaking into the telephone.

"Now, Mother," Mr. Kranik said. "You've checked everything of Steve's a dozen times. We must be on our way. Remember, I've got to get Steve and Tim to Springfield before ten o'clock." He looked at his son. "Ready, Steve? We'd better go."

Cathy, following a "Good-by," which had a choked-up sound to it, put down the telephone. The call had been from Tim. She had hoped very hard that he would call, and he had.

"Just called to say a special 'Good-by' to you, Cathy. Maybe you would write to me in the Navy?" he had said.

[ *21* ]

*Steve threw his arms around his mother*

"Oh, I will, Tim. I will," Cathy had promised.

"Steve and your father about ready to leave?"

"Any minute. Right away now."

"Well, good-by, then."

"Good-by."

The moment had arrived. It was July 5, 1957, the day Steve and Tim would actually enter the Navy. Behind them were all the preliminaries, the tests, the various forms filled out, papers signed, Navy investigations made.

This was the big day, the first of many big days Steve and Tim were going to have.

Steve closed his suitcase and walked toward the kitchen door. He dropped the bag in the middle of the kitchen and threw his arm around his mother. Tears were streaming down her face. Cathy's eyes were filled with tears, too. Billy and Mary, upset without knowing why, joined in with tears and howls, but still held on to their slices of bread and jam. Mr. Kranik stood in the doorway. He had to swallow hard to choke back the lump that had come into his throat.

The farewells were over. Steve's father backed the car out of the garage into the street as the rest of the Kranik family stood in the front yard, waving.

[ *23* ]

Mr. Kranik was driving the boys to Springfield to the enlistment center, the same place to which Steve and Tim had gone a few weeks before for the physical examinations and other tests. Tim's father worked during the daytime, and since Mr. Kranik was still on the night shift at Electric Boat, it had been decided that he would take the boys.

Much the same scene was being played at the Borden home when Steve and his father pulled up in front and honked the horn.

Moments later, Tim, his mother, and his father appeared on the front porch and came out to the car.

Tim gave his mother a bear hug.

"Don't cry, Mom. I'm not going away forever. We just have nine weeks in boot camp, then we come home for a few days."

"I know. I know, Tim. But you've never been away that long before. And you will be careful, won't you?"

"Sure, Mom, sure." Tim turned to his father. They shook hands. Tim lowered his head, as the parting handshake ended. He didn't want his father to see the tears in his eyes.

"By, son," Mrs. Borden said briskly before her voice could break. "Take care."

Mr. Kranik put the car into gear. Tim's parents waved as the boys and Mr. Kranik started down the street.

They were on their way to Springfield and their first day in the United States Navy. They were on their way to take part in an adventure that would startle the world.

# CHAPTER THREE

## *Trial by Fire*

---

TIM and Steve were walking across the parade ground of the United States Naval Training Station at Bainbridge, Maryland, where they were taking their boot training.

"Are you as scared as I am?" Steve asked his friend.

"Who, me? Scared! That's a laugh," Tim replied. "Ha-ha-ha. See, I've proved it to you."

Steve ignored Tim's attempt at a joke. "But what they told us today. I mean about how bad a fire on shipboard can be. I'm scared of fire. Any kind of fire."

Tim didn't reply at once. He cast a glance at his friend. Steve's mouth was set in grim, stern lines. Tim knew from that expression that Steve might be frightened, but he was also determined. And when Steve had his mind made up, he would face anything.

"Look, Steve. Of course, I'm scared. Who wouldn't be? I'm really a lot more afraid of this deal we've got to go through than you are, and you know it."

Steve didn't know it. Of the two boys, Tim had always been the more daring, the more reckless. Tim was always ready to take a chance, to accept a challenge. It was Tim's colorful imagination that sometimes made him see danger that didn't exist.

To Steve, a situation was either scary, or it wasn't. He didn't dream up perils that didn't exist. If any situation presented danger, Steve thought it over for a moment or two, gulped down the beginnings of any fright, then faced up to it. He might say he was scared, but what he really meant was that he wasn't afraid of the situation itself, but of how he himself might behave in it.

"You listen to those other trainees, though, and it makes you wonder," Steve said.

"Oh, sure. But they've been through it. They just want to show us how brave they were and toss a scare into us at the same time."

The situation the boys were discussing was the

[ 27 ]

three-day "trial by fire" which the trainees in Perry Regiment would be facing, starting the following morning. Tim and Steve were in Perry Regiment.

For several days, trainees who had already gone through the ordeal had taunted members of Perry Regiment with the cry:

"You'll be sorr . . . ee!"

Classroom work to prepare for the fire fighting drills had ended that afternoon. For two days, the boys had heard nothing but "fire," "fire," "fire," from their instructors. The devastation of a raging fire on shipboard had been pounded and pounded into them until they even dreamed of fire. And always, every instructor ended his lecture or demonstration with the fearful sounding sentence:

"Remember this—if a ship catches on fire, there's *no place to go!*"

Tomorrow started the three-day "ordeal by fire," for trainees Tim Borden and Steve Kranik.

The first weeks of boot training for the boys had sped by as an ever-changing, never-ending wonder of new experiences in an exciting, different world. They had slipped quickly and easily into the daily routine. They were up each morning at five. They worked hard until four in the afternoon when the day's instruction officially ended. At nine-thirty, it was "Lights out!" Another day of training was behind them.

Their bodies had become hardened from the physical training and daily sports. Tim, taller than Steve, had filled out. His shoulders had grown broader and more powerful. Stocky Steve had put on weight at first from three plentiful meals a day plus nightly stops at the Navy Exchange for a "going-to-bed" snack. The excess weight melted away after the first two weeks as the training pace stepped up.

On Sunday, when the boys put on their Navy whites, they made a handsome pair. Tim was tall and rangy. His dark skin had become even darker, tanned by the hot sun during outdoor activities. Steve, half a head shorter, was fair, and the sun only reddened his fair skin.

"Good thing you're going to be in subs," Tim kidded his friend. "Sun can't get to you there. If you were on an aircraft carrier, you'd be as red as a lobster."

The boys were approaching their company barracks. It was a little after four o'clock. They had just completed two days of intensive classroom work in preparation for the three days of firefighting drills that would start in the morning.

They had learned about the chemistry of fire, so they would know the nature of various kinds of fires, raging oil fires, gasoline fires, fires from escaping gas. After two days they were thoroughly familiar with every type of the Navy's highly specialized fire-fighting equipment.

Passing the barracks next to their own, Tim and Steve watched a group of grimy, sooty-faced trainees come straggling along. Their fatigue uniforms were drenched.

"Boy, look at them," Tim said.

"Yeah. They've sure had it."

"And it's over for them."

"Wish it were for us," Steve said.

"Oh, forget it, Stevie. Come on. Let's take a swim."

They ran into their barracks, changed into swim trunks, and headed for the regiment's pool.

The next morning Tim, Steve, and other members of their platoon marched to the Damage Control Area. They were wearing "foul-weather" clothing, heavy slickers treated to resist heat and flame. Hoods of the same material were worn low over their faces. Heavy gloves protected their hands.

In the area was an oblong structure built to

resemble the engine room of a ship. On each side were two small doors, exactly like the iron doors leading into a ship's boiler or engine room.

"That the one we're going to hit today?"

The boy asking the question was a friend of Tim's and Steve's called Ski. His last name was Manowski. In the Navy, anyone whose name ended in the letters, *ski* or *sky*, was automatically called "Ski."

"Gee, I don't know, Ski," Tim said. "If not today, then we'll have to hit it tomorrow."

The group was called to attention and marched to a round, open tank.

"Looks to me like this is the one we'll start on," Steve said.

In the distance, about one hundred yards away, they could see the third object which would be used to demonstrate their skill at fire fighting. This looked like an airplane that had crashed.

All three of these "mock-ups"—structures built to look like the real thing—would be drenched with oil and high-test gasoline and ignited. It was the job of the fire fighters to put out the roaring infernos and to put them out fast.

"All right, men. This is it." The chief petty officer in charge called the group to attention.

"You've been told what to expect. In a few minutes, this tank, half full of gasoline, will be set on fire. You're to put it out, and pronto! It's *got* to be fast. If this tank were on a ship, and the fire wasn't controlled in minutes, the whole ship would go up."

There was restless, uncertain movement among the platoon. The young trainees looked quickly at one another. Some pulled their hoods more tightly over their faces.

"Man the hose!"

Tim, Steve, and eight others raised the four-inch, heavy hose they stood alongside. Tim had the nozzle.

The nozzle was specially built to allow the fire fighter to shoot out a powerful, heavy spray or a fine mist.

Behind Tim and Steve's group, but out of its vision was a stand-by unit. They were veterans, skilled fire fighters ready to take over the moment anything went wrong or got out of control.

A Damage Controlman 1st Class approached the tank. He tossed a flaming brand over its edge. There was a low "Baroooom!" which shook the ground as the gasoline exploded, and flames shot twenty feet above the top of the tank.

"Fog the deck!" the chief shouted.

Tim turned the nozzle of the hose toward the ground. This was the first step. The spray must be controlled from the moment the nozzle is turned on. By aiming the nozzle at the ground, the direction of the spray can be controlled.

"Hit the nozzle!"

Tim's left hand slashed at the lever that released the spray.

"Raise hose!"

The ten trainees took a firmer grip of the heavy tubing.

"Attack!"

With Tim in the lead, Steve right behind him, the hose was advanced toward the flaming tank.

Slowly they worked up. With every foot advanced, the heat became more and more intense. Tim, in the lead, took the brunt of it. For a moment, he didn't think he could stand it, and nearly panicked. He felt Steve's body press against him.

"Good old Steve," Tim thought, and gained strength and courage from the nearness of his friend.

Two more steps nearer the tank's side. The spray mist was taking effect. The flames seemed to retreat, and the heat became less intense.

At the side of the tank, which came up to Tim's waist, he pointed the nozzle over the rim. The

men behind him raised the hose above their heads. Tim swung the nozzle back and forth in a small area until the flames were extinguished. Then he widened the arc of the spray, increasing and thickening the mist until it became a direct stream of anti-gasoline liquid.

This action enabled Tim to reach the far side of the tank. He whipped the stream back and forth, back and forth, confining the fire, reducing its size until he could direct the powerful spray on a smaller, more compact body of flame.

Now and again, a burning splash would re-ignite a section of the tank already extinguished. Quickly Tim directed the spray at the new flame, putting it out.

At last, after what seemed to Tim to be hours, only a small circle of flame still burned.

"Got you! Got you!" Tim yelled as if he were conquering a human enemy.

He directed the stream at the circle of fire. Out it went.

Quickly Tim readjusted the nozzle to spray mist and laid a thin cover of mist over the whole tank.

"Last man back!" he shouted.

He felt a tug from behind. His order had been for the end man on the hose to start walking slowly backward. In this way, the hose could be removed in an orderly manner. There would be no danger of anyone stumbling over the hose. The group moved back from the tank in the same well-drilled, careful manner in which they had approached it.

"Lower hose."

The tired group gratefully laid the hose on the ground.

"Good work," the chief called out. "You almost beat the record."

"How long did it take, Chief?" one of the trainees asked.

"Nine minutes, twenty-three seconds."

Tim was astounded. It had taken less than ten minutes to put out that blazing inferno. He felt as if he had been fighting the fire all day.

The second day, Tim and Steve's group fought a fire in the structure built to resemble an engine room. Two teams worked this fire, one from each side of the "engine room." The job here was to contain the fire, drive it into a corner, then extinguish it. The test went smoothly. The fire was put out quickly.

"Two down, one to go," Tim said to Steve, a broad grin on his sooty face. "Still scared?"

Steve shrugged his shoulders. "Not as much as

I was before. I still don't like fires, though."

"Who does, in the Navy or out?"

The third and final day of fire fighting found the platoon from Perry Regiment at the mock-up of an aircraft. It was nosed over as if it had crashed while landing on an aircraft carrier.

The plane was ignited.

"Hit the nozzle! Attack!" came the shouted orders.

The group moved in on the flaming "plane."

The heat was terrific. A slight wind bent the flames in the direction of the attacking fire fighters.

Tim and Steve were end men in this test. The nozzle carrier swept the plane from nose to tail with a heavy spray. The group closed in. Now a fine mist was shot out over the whole plane. The fire was extinguished.

A cheer went up.

"Good work. You've tied the record," the chief said.

"Lower hose."

In the pleased excitement of tying the record for speed in putting out the plane fire, the nozzle holder became careless. He dropped the nozzle instead of placing it carefully on the ground. In doing so, the release lever was sprung open. The full force of the spray shot out at the group.

"Wild hose! Wild hose!"

This cry was as terrifying to the trainees and instructors as the dreaded cry of "Fire!"

The hose lashed back and forth like a boa constrictor. Spray shot into the eyes of the trainees, blinding them. Once the lethal hose swung in a wide, sweeping arc, striking a group of trainees at ankle height. They toppled over as if cut down by a giant scythe.

"Come on, Steve!" Tim shouted. He made a dash for the nozzle end of the hose, now lashing back and forth in short, wicked strokes. The ground was muddy and slippery.

As Tim neared the nozzle, he dived through the air, his body landing on top of the hose, his hands grabbing frantically at the nozzle. Steve hit the hose right behind Tim. The weight of their bodies finally subdued the writhing, four-inch monster.

Tim found the release catch and forced it closed. The danger was over. Tim and Steve still lay atop the hose, breathless, almost exhausted.

The chief petty officer in command came running up.

"That was a brave act you two pulled off!" he exclaimed. "I'll see that it's written up in your record. You'll receive an official commendation for bravery."

Tim looked at Steve and grinned. Both boys made the "V" for victory sign with their fingers.

# CHAPTER FOUR

## *Down the Hatch*

---

THE pride of the United States Navy's submarine fleet lay at her mooring, Pier 91, in Seattle, Washington. She was the U.S.S. *Nautilus,* the world's first atomic-powered submarine.

Taking their off-duty ease in the Crew's Mess were Tim Borden and Steve Kranik, the two newest members of the ship's crew of 116 officers and men. Steve was standing by the juke box, snapping his fingers and moving his shoulders in rhythm to the bouncy music the machine was spinning out. Tim was turning the pages of a textbook on electronics, a subject he had become more and more interested in.

Two other crewmen were playing a game of acey-deucy. Two more were engaged in a serious battle of cribbage.

"Hey, Kranik," one of the cribbage players called. "How about knocking it off for a while? You've played that same record six times."

"At your service," Steve grinned in reply. "Anything you say."

The song ended. Steve looked over at Tim. It seemed to Steve that Tim had his head buried in books most of the time these days.

"Gotta break that up," he said to himself, "Or that boy is going to be an electrified genius."

He crossed over to the Coke machine, took out a chill, moisture-beaded bottle, and moved over to sit down by his friend.

"Hey, Tim," he said. "How about laying off the brainstuffing for a while. Remember, we were going to do a tape to send Cathy."

Tim closed his book and smiled back at Steve.

"Okay. No time like the present."

"I'll set up the tape-recorder. You do the talking," Steve said.

"We'll both do the talking," Tim replied.

Tim and Steve had joined the crew of the *Nautilus* only a few weeks before. This was their first cruise aboard the Navy's finest underseas craft. On their departure from New London for the West Coast by way of the Panama Canal, the boys had promised to send Cathy, and through her, their families, a full description of life aboard a nuclear-powered submarine. It had been Cathy's idea to buy the supply of mailing tapes— short tapes already in a box, easy to mail. "Write? Huh!" she had said. "I know you two. You're allergic to pens and stationery. Since you like to shoot the breeze so much, just shoot it onto this tape and send it along home."

Steve had the tape-recorder set up in one corner of the room. He threaded the tape carefully into it, tested it briefly, then called out, "All set, Tim."

Tim came over to the machine.

"You talk first," Steve said.

"Hunh-unh. Not me. You first."

"Okay, okay, all ready. What do I talk about?"

"Tell her what this submarine looks like."

Steve cleared his throat several times, then snapped the recorder on.

"Hello, Cathy," he began, grinning. "This is Steve—your brother. This big lug Tim is here with me. You were right; this beats writing. We're making this tape recording to tell you about the *Nautilus*. Sis, she's really a great ship. The greatest. And big, too, plenty big. From her bow to her stern, she measures 320 feet—that's longer than a football field. She's 28 feet in diameter—that means from her keel to her deck, from top to bottom. Ahemmm . . . I hope I'm coming through to you loud and clear . . . I'll turn this over to Tim now . . ."

"Hi, Cathy." Tim took the hand mike from Steve. "We had a great trip out from New London. Through the Panama Canal, up the coast of California with a call at San Francisco. There's a town you want to see some day, Cathy—"

"Tell her about the sub—not sightseeing in 'Frisco'," Steve hissed.

Tim glowered at Steve, then continued.

"We're cutting this tape in the Crew's Mess. It's a big room, lots bigger than the Mess on the *Conger,* the sub we were on before. That's because the *Conger* had to carry a large battery and tons and tons of Diesel oil—those two things alone take up half the space on a conventional, fleet-type sub like the *Conger.* That's why this room is almost four times as large as the Crew's Mess on the old *Conger.* . . ."

"Tell her some of the things we have in here," Steve whispered.

*"Hi, Cathy." Tim took the hand mike from Steve*

"Here are some of the things we have in this room: a Coke machine and an ice-cream machine —that's where your brother spends most of his time. We also have a built-in hi-fi system, a record player, a juke box—five tunes for a nickel —and this tape recorder, of course. Then, to make it easy for us, the *Nautilus* has an automatic washer and dryer, a nucleonics lab, complete machine shop, a dark room for developing pictures, and a big library. Don't you feel sorry for us? We really have it tough, don't we? Well, now I'll turn this back to Steve."

Tim stopped the recorder as he handed the mike over to Steve. "Tell her about bumping your head the other night," Tim prompted.

Steve grinned and took the mike.

"Tim says to tell you how we sleep. He's an expert at putting in *sack* time. That means he's good at sleeping. Well, no one would ever call our bunks the last word in luxury. But they are comfortable. Only thing is, once you get stretched out in one of them, there's only about eight inches of space from the top of your forehead to the bottom of the bunk above you. The other night, I was dreaming or something and sat up too fast. Bango—I saw plenty of stars. It was okay though, about the stars, I mean, since it was night—"

"Very funny, vereee funny," Tim cut in.

"One thing Tim forgot to tell you. This Crew's Mess can be changed into a movie theater in about two minutes flat. We have movies every day and good ones, too. Join the Navy and see the movies. Here, I'm giving this back to Tim."

"Your brother's a real comic," Tim said. "I don't know what more to tell you. The food's good. Best food in the Navy. And plenty of it. When we're on duty, we just wear dungarees or work clothes. So do the officers. Only difference is they wear the insignia indicating their rank on the points of their collars. If you want to know something about what makes an atomic-powered sub run, I'll turn you back to Steve. He's the one who's really interested in nuclear propulsion . . . Here, Steve."

"Well, sis, it's like this . . ." Steve cleared his throat. He was going to show off his great wisdom. "This nuclear stuff is really very interesting. It's kind of hard to explain, but I'll try. The nuclear stuff—I mean the material that makes atomic power—it's in a lower deck, and we're protected from radiation by a thick flooring of lead and polyethylene. There are some pumps down there, too. These pumps move water through a reactor where the water picks up the heat of the controlled nuclear fission. This heat boils the water into steam. The steam goes to two turbines, or engines. They drive our two nine-foot propellers. That's what makes us go. Got that, sis? If not, I'll send you a diagram. Now, this is Steve Kranik, returning you to your local announcer. Take it away, Tim Borden."

"Thank you, Stephen Kranik. This is Tim Borden once again. Please say hello for me to my mom and dad, and hello to your folks, too, Cathy. Signing off now. Love and kisses."

Steve snatched the mike from Tim's hand.

"Same goes for me, Cathy. Write us. Lots of letters."

The boys unreeled the tape and put it in the mailing box.

"How'd it go? All right, you think?" Steve asked.

"Better than all right. Now the whole world can learn how a nuclear reactor on a submarine works. Hope no spies ever listen in."

"Aw, come off it, Tim. I did the best I could."

"I'm just kidding, Steve," Tim said. Steve's face really did have a crestfallen expression. "Don't look so shook. You're really learning your stuff in the engine room."

"Hey, you guys!" An acey-deucy player called out. He had been eavesdropping while Tim and Steve recorded. "You know, you told her everything about this here submarine except one thing."

"What's that?" Tim asked seriously.

"You didn't tell them about the leak we got in the basement."

"Gee, that's right, Tim." Steve said. "I forgot all about it. Give the folks a laugh. Here we got a million-dollar home, and the basement leaks!"

The *Nautilus* did have a leak. It was a small one, but a serious one. The crew joked about it, but they knew how dangerous it could be.

"Tell you what," Steve said, with a sparkle of fun in his eyes. "I bet I could fix that leak."

"You! And just what would you do?" a cribbage player exploded. "Sailor, this sub's been gone over by experts."

"Sure, I know. But I've fixed leaks before. Just like this one."

The other men in the room leaned forward, half skeptical, half believing.

"Sure. Now just tell us, Mr. Leak Fixer 3rd Class, how would you fix that leak?"

Steve grinned. "I'd get some of that stuff they put in leaking car radiators. That would stop it."

"Ooohh, brother!" the men yelled in chorus.

Steve ducked just in time to miss a barrage of magazines hurled at his grinning face.

# CHAPTER FIVE

*Operation Stop Leak*

---

DIRECTLY above the Crew's Mess, where Tim and Steve had recorded their tape to Cathy, was the Officers' Wardroom. Just off the Wardroom, the captain of the *Nautilus,* Commander William R. Anderson, sat at his desk behind the locked door of his small stateroom.

Captain Anderson was the only man on board —officer or crewman—who knew that within a few days the *Nautilus* might cast off for a daring, dangerous cruise that, if successful, would thrill the entire world. Commander Anderson was sweating it out—waiting for top secret orders that would tell him to put Operation Sunshine into immediate effect or—to cancel it.

The captain toyed with two sets of operation orders. One was stamped "Confidential." The other set was labeled with the exciting words: "Top Secret—Eyes only of the Commanding Officer."

The orders directing him to put one or the other of the two orders into operation could come at any minute.

Elsewhere in the ship, the officers and crew were going about their duties in preparation for what they believed was to be a southern voyage. They couldn't have been more wrong.

Not, of course, that it mattered to any of that underwater craft's fine crew. They had complete confidence in the *Nautilus* and in her skipper. It most certainly didn't matter to Tim and Steve. Their dream had come true. After weeks and months of schooling and six months on the U.S.S. *Conger,* a diesel-powered fleet submarine, they were at long last part of the crew of the nuclear-powered *Nautilus.*

Tim and Steve looked up as Chief Stuart Nelson came in the Crew's Mess.

"I want six men," he said, looking about the room. "And here you are. An even half dozen. Aren't you the lucky ones!"

The men groaned. Here went their off-duty ease.

"You, Borden, and you, Kranik. Higgins, Smith, Yuill and Lynch. Got a job for you."

The chief began his briefing, describing the job. As he progressed, five pairs of eyes focused on Steve. It couldn't be, the expressions in those eyes seemed to say. This was really the craziest! That nutty idea Steve had mentioned only a few minutes earlier—certainly no one would give it serious consideration. Not the skipper, nor the engineering officer. But one of them had—one of them must have had the same idea about the time Steve had mentioned it in a kidding way.

"Now here's some dough for each of you," Chief Nelson was saying. "Get as much of the stuff as you can. The skipper wants plenty of it."

He distributed the money to the six men.

"Okay now. When you go ashore, wear your civvies, your civilian clothes. And this is a very, *very* hush-hush deal. Not a word of this is to leak —" the chief paused to correct himself. The word "leak" wasn't a good one to use on the *Nautilus*. "Not a word of this is to get out. It may sound like a crazy idea, but if the skipper wants to try it, that's going to be all right with all of us. Get me?"

The men "got" him.

"And another thing. Don't let anyone know you're from the *Nautilus*. Boy, they'd really think we're nuts if they knew you guys were on a submarine. That's all. Dismissed."

Half an hour later the six sailors, dressed in their "civvies" came up through the sub's forward hatch and went ashore.

"Boy, oh boy," Smith said. "I've put in lots of time in this man's navy, but this assignment is the craziest yet."

"Me, too. I've had some screwball duties tossed at me, but this one's got more curves than a movie queen."

Steve looked smugly at Tim, a "what-did-I-tell you-expression" on his face.

The men moved as a group along the dock toward the street.

"Sailor," said Lynch, the oldest man in the group, turning to Steve, "you weren't just kidding awhile ago when you were telling us you knew how to stop that leak."

"Leak Expert 3rd Class, that's me," Steve replied.

"Aren't we being modest!" Tim said, trying to take Steve down a peg. "Now you know darn well you were just joking when you said you thought that stuff to stop leaks in car radiators might work."

"The captain thinks so, too, doesn't he?" Tim could only shrug his shoulders.

"If he didn't, then why is he sending us out to buy all the 'Stop Leak' we can find in Seattle?"

"Stop Leak" is a commercial preparation poured into the radiators of automobiles with minor leaks.

"Well, I don't know, Steve. Maybe it could work on the *Nautilus*. Nothing else has."

The *Nautilus*, the finest submarine ever built, costing more than $100,000,000, had developed two leaks on its voyage from New London, through the Panama Canal, and up the west coast to Seattle.

A leak in any ship is a serious matter. But a leak in a submarine can be frightening, even though the crew jokes about it. The jokes would have been fewer if the crew had known the secret cruise planned for the *Nautilus*.

The plans for the *Nautilus* were important ones. Months and months of secret, top level work had gone into the daring voyage proposed for the sub. A tiny leak could cancel those plans.

One of the leaks had been corrected shortly after its discovery. This leak was in the number one periscope. The packing around the periscope, to keep the water out, had been faulty. Salt water had trickled down the scope and on down the neck of the officer or crewman using it.

The packing had been replaced, and the periscope no longer leaked.

The other leak, though, was far more serious. It was a small one, so small it was believed not to be any larger than a human hair. But, small though it was, it permitted salt water from one of the steam condensers to drip on an important part of machinery. If the leak wasn't located, it could, in time, be the cause of a serious breakdown in the propulsion machinery, the machinery that drove the submarine.

Engineering officers and teams of experts flown in from all over the country tried to find the leak. As Electrician's Mates, 3rd Class, both Tim and Steve worked along with the experts.

They went over every tube and pipe they could reach.

"How many tubes and pipes you figure this underwater seegar has in her?" Steve asked Tim. Both were helpers on a team of experts going over the steam condensers for the fiftieth time.

"More'n enough to build a jungle gym for every playground in the U. S. and A." Tim replied.

"You're not far from right there, m'lad," one

of the experts cut in. "That leak could be in any one of ten thousand places, and a lot more we can't get at without taking a can opener and ripping this sub apart."

The leak hadn't been found by the time the *Nautilus* came to rest at her mooring in Seattle Harbor.

Commander Anderson was becoming more and more worried. Knowing, as he did, about the proposed plans for the undersea craft, he realized that unless the leak were discovered and checked, orders could come winging through at any time calling the whole project off.

That was when he called in his Engineering Officer, Lieutenant Commander Paul Early, and proposed the fantastic idea of using "Stop Leak," a fluid to pour into leaky auto radiators.

The six sailors separated when they reached downtown Seattle.

"Guess we better fan out," one said. "We don't all want to hit the same area. Wouldn't look so good."

"And I don't think we should buy more than two, maybe four quarts at the most in any one filling station," Tim suggested. "What do you think?"

"Check, matey. You got a good idea there."

By nightfall the "Stop Leak" task force returned to the *Nautilus* with 140 quart cans of the liquid.

The entire crew of the sub stood by in solemn silence as the "Stop Leak" was poured into the sub's condenser system. Breathless moments went by.

Tim looked at Steve, shrugging his shoulders in a question.

Steve grinned back and crossed his fingers.

Twenty minutes passed. Some of the crew, restless with the waiting, wandered back to the Crew's Mess. Coffee was sipped in silence. Someone turned on the juke box.

"Shut that thing off," snapped a chief.

Half an hour later, Commander Early, standing by the machine on which the water had been dripping, shook his head.

"I can't believe it." His expression of astonishment turned to one of wonder and pleasure as the dripping stopped. A cheer went up from those who had stayed with him.

From all over the sub, crewmen and officers crowded into the engine room.

Cheers broke out.

A hundred-million-dollar nuclear-powered submarine had been repaired by "Stop Leak," costing $1.80 a quart!

After chow that night, Steve came up to Tim with a happy look on his face.

"Know what, Tim? We get shore leave tonight. Because we helped get the 'Stop Leak.' How 'bout that?"

Tim's answer was a frown.

"Well, what are you waiting for?" Steve demanded. "Get your cap, and let's shove off."

"I don't think I will tonight, Steve."

"Why not? You and the captain going to hold a conference?" Steve asked, kidding his friend. "There's a good movie playing. You know, that one with Gary Cooper you've been wanting to see."

"No, Steve, I've got something else to do."

"Like what? Come on. What's eating you, Tim?"

"Look, Steve. You go on. I told you I got something else to do."

"Something else? Something you can't tell me? Me, your old buddy Steve?"

A serious note came into Tim's voice, and a

frown crossed his face. "Yes, something I can't tell you. Now leave me alone, will you?"

Tim turned and walked away. Steve watched him go, his face a picture of amazement. What had gotten into Tim? He had never acted this way before.

# CHAPTER SIX

## *Operation Sunshine*

---

THE next morning, Steve, still worried and puzzled by his friend's strange actions of the night before, sought Tim out.

"Hey, what was eating you last night?" Steve demanded.

"Oh, nothing," Tim replied evasively.

"Now don't be giving me that 'oh, nothing' routine. What was it?"

"Look, Steve," Tim said seriously, "I don't want to talk about it. Let's just forget it. You don't have to know everything I'm doing, do you?"

A hurt look came over Steve's face. He started to say something, then closed his lips tightly to hold back an angry reply, turned, and walked away. Tim, a flash of unhappiness crossing his face, shrugged his shoulders.

[ *63* ]

*"Hey, what was eating you last night?" Steve demanded*

For the next two days the boys didn't see much of one another. They were standing different watches. Tim was asleep when Steve was on duty, and when both were awake and off duty together, few words passed between them.

As much as Steve liked his friend, he had his pride.

"Darned if I'm going to push him," Steve told himself. "If he wants to be all mysterious and hold out on me, then I'll just wait until he gets over it and finally tells me about it."

That's how Steve decided to let matters rest. That is, until mail call that day.

It was June 8, 1958. At mail call there were two letters for Steve. One was from his mother, the other from his sister Cathy. His mother's letter was the usual bright, cheery, newsy letter. All about the kids, his young brother Billy, and his other sister Mary. School would soon be out, and the youngsters were getting excited about vacation time.

Mary had received her birthday present from Steve and was so proud of it. Steve had sent it to her from the Panama Canal Zone. "She was so excited to get a present mailed from out of the country," Mrs. Kranik wrote.

Cathy's letter, though, brought a worried look to Steve's face. He took his mail and crawled into his bunk. He reread Cathy's letter twice. He could tell that Cathy was trying not to worry him too much. But the facts were there, no escaping their meaning. And those facts might mean the end of Steve's navy career.

Steve got out of his bunk. A thought had come to him. Maybe Tim had had a letter from Cathy a day or two before. Perhaps Tim knew the situation back in New London. Perhaps that was why Tim had suddenly begun acting so strangely.

Steve found Tim forward in the torpedo room.

"Want to talk to you for a minute, Tim," Steve said.

"Okay, fire away."

"Did you get a letter from Cathy recently? In the last couple of days?"

Before Tim could reply, the boys heard a click that told them the ship's public address system had been turned on.

"All hands! All hands!" came the voice through the loud-speaker. "Report immediately to the Crew's Mess for pre-underway briefing."

There was a scramble as men from all sections of the ship piled into the Crew's Mess. The briefing by the Executive Officer was short and to the point. The *Nautilus* was to get underway as quickly as possible. They would be informed as to their destination once they were at sea.

In his stateroom, Captain Anderson wore a big smile on his face. The orders had come through. They were the ones he had been hoping for—a three-word message: "EXECUTE OPERATION SUNSHINE."

The long-planned, daring voyage had now become a reality. It had been code-named "Sunshine" to mislead anyone as to exactly where the *Nautilus* was headed. Who would ever associate the word "sunshine" with the cold, forbidding wastelands of the Arctic?

The activities and the pace of the crew stepped up for the rest of the day. There was no time for Steve to question Tim any further.

When a ship or submarine puts out to sea for a lengthy cruise, there are a million and one last-minute details to attend to. Last-minute supplies are loaded: medical supplies, steaks, fresh fruit, chili peppers, carbon dioxide for the Coke machine.

The check list of items is long and carefully prepared.

"Check off the aspirin."

"Aye, aye, sir."

"Film . . . radishes . . . typewriter ribbons . . . torpedo alcohol . . . coffee . . . oxygen . . . rags . . . transistors . . . salt . . . soap . . ."

All day long, supplies of every description poured into the *Nautilus,* each item carefully checked off as it went down the hatches of the submarine.

At 0024 hours—24 minutes after midnight—on June 9, 1958, the engineering officer Paul Early reported to the captain:

"Ready to get underway, sir."

The captain took a final careful look around.

"Take in all lines," he ordered. "All back two thirds."

The *Nautilus* backed away from its mooring. She was on her history-making way.

As the sleek submarine slipped through the choppy waters of Puget Sound in the dark, starless night, Tim and Steve found themselves assigned to a puzzling detail.

They were with a gang on the main deck painting over the white identifying numbers of the Nautilus—571—on her bow and sail or conning tower.

"What's the idea of this, I wonder?" Tim asked

"You got me," Steve said, slapping some gray paint over the numeral "7."

"I guess somebody must not want anyone to know where we're going or who we are," Tim speculated.

Tim was exactly right. The mission was Top Secret. Orders had been given that the *Nautilus* was to make every effort to remain undetected, and if detected, to make it impossible to identify the ship. That was why the numbers 571 were being painted over. The paint would dry while the *Nautilus* remained on the surface, running out of Puget Sound.

"I thought we were going to Panama," one of the paint detail said.

"That's what I heard."

"Then why all the mystery?"

"The Navy likes to confuse us."

"That's because we're in it."

"I hope we do go to Panama. I put a deposit down on a camera. Don't want to lose it."

It would be a long time before the men got back to the Canal Zone.

The painting detail was over. The men went down the hatch. Some went to the coffee machine, always ready at any hour of the day or night. Several of the crew still lounged around in the Mess. All were keyed up. This happened every time the

*Nautilus* put out to sea. Although by now casting off for a voyage was old stuff for the crew, the excitement of a new voyage never failed to stir the men.

There was still speculation about where the ship was heading. Panama . . . across the Equator in the Pacific . . . routine cruise . . . joining the Pacific fleet for maneuvers. All these destinations were voiced by various crew members.

Then came the click of the public address system. A quick silence settled over the ship.

"All hands. This is the Captain speaking. Our destination for this trip is Portland, England, via the North Pole . . ."

For a few moments the crew was stunned by the news.

"England! By the North Pole! That means under ice most of the way!"

"Never been done before!"

"Over the top of the world!"

"But *under* it, you mean."

"We'll be the first submarine to reach the North Pole . . ."

"If we make it."

"What do you mean, *if* we make it!"

"We'll make it, all right."

"Crikey! am I ever glad I saved those two British pound notes."

"You're glad! I still got some Panamanian money left. Lot of good it'll do me now."

"Quit griping. Don't you want to be in the history books, sailor?"

Tim and Steve exchanged happy smiles. Members of the crew of the *Nautilus* only a few weeks, and here they were, on a voyage that, if successful, would truly make history.

The *Nautilus,* still on the surface, plowed steadily through the waters of the Sound.

She was ice-pack bound!

# CHAPTER SEVEN

## Ice Pack Bound

THE *Nautilus,* flying no colors and with no identifying numerals, had to play hide and seek as she
steamed out of Puget Sound. An unidentified submarine could cause plenty of excitement if spotted
by other naval craft or from the air.

Tim was on the forenoon watch that first day
out. He came on duty at 0800 hours—8:00 A.M.
—and would go off duty at 1200 hours—noon.

His duty this morning was in the control room.
The officer of the Deck kept him busy calling for
a change in course time after time to dodge and
keep well clear of merchant shipping.

At 0900, an hour after Tim came on duty, the
*Nautilus* cleared the Strait of Juan de Fuca, just a
few miles off Swiftsure Lightship.

*Tim's duty this morning was in the control room*

The sub's klaxon sounded twice.

"Ah—ooga . . . Ah—ooga." The signal to submerge.

In moments, the *Nautilus* plunged under the sea. A feeling of relief swept through the entire crew. The submarine was in her true element now. She wasn't built to run on the surface. Everyone in the crew liked it much better when the ship was underwater.

Ballast was trimmed. The *Nautilus* dived deeper into the ocean. At three hundred feet below, she was leveled off. Her speed was increased to more than twenty knots. Her needle-like bow was pointed toward the Bering Strait.

Coming off duty at noon, Tim felt exhausted. He had been up late, long after midnight, caught up in the duties and the excitement of sailing. He'd had only three hours sleep before standing his forenoon watch.

Tim headed for the crew's sleeping quarters, with but one thought in his mind—sleep. As he passed through the Crew's Mess, Steve called to him.

"Hey, Tim. Want to talk to you."

Tim didn't reply. He just shook his head and

[ *75* ]

ducked through the oval-shaped doorway leading toward the torpedo room.

Not understanding that Tim's refusal to stop and talk was mainly because he was so tired, Steve decided then and there to skip the talk he wanted to have with his friend. Maybe Tim had heard from Cathy. Maybe he did know about the situation in New London. But, Steve told himself, if he did, then he, Tim, would have to be the first one to mention it. Steve wasn't going to bring it up. It seemed to Steve that the break between him and Tim was widening. He shook his head, unable to puzzle it out.

In the Crew's Mess the tension and excitement seemed to increase with each mile the *Nautilus* steamed nearer the North Pole. Charts were brought out. A larger polar map was hung in the Mess, and every few hours the position of the submarine was plotted and marked on the map.

A new friend of Steve's was one of the leaders in this activity. He hadn't been on the *Nautilus* much longer than Tim and Steve, but he acted as if he personally ran the sub most of the time. He did this in a nice way. He was a friendly fellow, and no one objected if he bragged too much. He was sort of a "wise guy" but a funny one. He was called "Radar" because he had big ears that stood out on each side of his head like the huge scoop-shaped antennae used in radar scanning.

"Hey, Stevie boy, come over here," Radar called. "I'll show you just exactly where we're going.

"You see, Stevie," he went on, "I just had a conference with the Skipper. He asks me, Radar, how to get to this Bering Strait we're headed for. Tell me, do you think we should ought to go through the front door or the back door?"

Steve knew, of course, that the only words exchanged between the Captain and Radar in the past forty-eight hours had been "Yes, sir," or "Ay, ay, sir." Radar knew that Steve knew this, but that didn't stop Radar.

"What's this business about doors?" Steve asked.

"Now I'm glad you asked me that, Stevie boy. I'm just the guy that can tell you all about it."

"Oh, sure. Is there anything you're not an expert on?"

"Very little, Steve, very little."

Radar was one of the group of crewmen already known as "Engine Room Navigators." This group spent most of its off-duty time hanging over the shoulder of the Navigator examining his chart and inspecting the course plotted for the *Nautilus*. This was how Radar had obtained his information about the "doors" to the Bering Strait.

There are what navigators call two doors to the strait. One of them is on the western side of St. Lawrence Island—a channel between the island and Siberia. The other channel, or door, is on the eastern side—between the island and Alaska.

Since the channel between Siberia and St. Lawrence Island is farther north than the eastern channel, Radar chose to call it the "back door," and the channel between the island and Alaska the "front door."

"You see, going to the North Pole this way," Radar said, pointing to the chart, "we're going to skirt around the western side of that St. Lawrence Island and use the 'back door.' Get it?"

"Looks to me like the 'front door' is nearer," Steve replied.

"Sure. Looks that way on the map. But on the Great Circle route"—here Radar put on his most solemn, wisest expression—"the Great Circle Route is actually the shorter way to the pole. And that's why we're heading for the 'back door.'"

"Aw, come off it, Radar." Another crewman

had joined in. "The real reason we're going to the west of the island is because the water's deeper there."

Radar put on a hurt expression. "But of course. I thought that was understood."

The crewman slapped Radar on the back and winked at Steve.

"This guy kills me," he said.

Steve looked up at the ship's clock.

"Jeepers!" he exclaimed. "I've got to go on duty in half an hour. And I wanted to catch a ration of sack time. Instead, I sit here listening to you talking about front and back doors in this man's ocean."

"You see? That's all the thanks I get," Radar said. But Steve had already gone. He could still get in fifteen fast minutes of sleep before he went on duty.

The *Nautilus* slid under the cold waters off the Aleutian Islands, drinking up the miles remaining between her and her destination—the North Pole.

Two hundred and fifty feet above the trim craft, a violent storm was raging. Thirty-foot waves, driven by a screaming, icy wind, lashed the ocean into a frenzied, frightening mass of troubled water.

The *Nautilus,* though, deep beneath this storm, rode as smoothly as if she were motionless. At her cruising depth, there was no sense or feeling of motion to the crew. It was as if they were home, sitting in front of the television in their living rooms. The water at the depth of 250 feet or more is as calm as an inland pond, no matter how severe a storm may be raging overhead.

This was the main reason the crew preferred cruising submerged. On the surface, the *Nautilus* would be tossed about by waves and storms just like any other ship. There were other comforts, too. The temperature was held at a steady 72 degrees, humidity 50 per cent. This temperature was maintained whether the *Nautilus* was cruising in the tropical waters of the Caribbean Sea or in the frigid waters of the Arctic Ocean.

"This is the life, the life for me

   Away, 'way down in the deep blue sea."

The crewman chanting the two-line verse was lounging on the small of his back, a plate of ice cream in one hand, a Coke in the other.

That night, at the showing of the first movie, one line brought a roar of laughter from the newer members of the *Nautilus'* crew. It was a picture about submarines, and the line that brought out the laughter was: "Who would have thought six months ago I would be on a submarine headed for the Artic?"

The next day, the atmosphere on the *Nautilus* grew more tense. The submarine encountered ice and trouble.

# CHAPTER EIGHT

## Depth Test

---

EVERYONE on board the *Nautilus* from her newest crew members—Tim and Steve—to the skipper, Commander Anderson, knew that the easy part of the voyage was over.

No one showed any doubts or fears for the success of the voyage. Spirits and confidence were still running high. But automatically everyone became more alert. Every task was performed with more care. There was less kidding around. This, the crew knew, was *it*. The dangerous part of the voyage through waters never traveled before was beginning.

The increased tension on the sub, the tightening up of every action, every duty, brought Steve and Tim back together. There still remained a certain amount of strain between them. Neither referred to the coolness which had recently developed. Both preferred to ignore it. The big problem right now was not their personal one. They were part of a team, a team that was undertaking a daring, highly dangerous adventure.

The *Nautilus* was a tight and happy ship. Discipline aboard, although never lax, became voluntarily tighter. The number of officers on duty for each watch was increased. The Executive Officer, Frank Adams, began a daily series of under-ice familiarization lectures. These lectures covered countless details to prepare the crew for anything likely to happen during the voyage. If unusual situations arose, the men would be prepared to handle them.

Special watches were trained in ice formation observation, temperature changes, and what to look for on the electronic instruments which told of the conditions ahead, above, and below the submarine.

On the third day out, the *Nautilus* left the warm waters of the Japanese current. There was a sudden drop in outside water temperature. The bathythermograph—an underwater thermometer—plunged down to 39 degrees Fahrenheit.

"All hands! All hands! Stand by for a depth test."

In moments the crew was at its emergency stations.

Tim and Steve stood side by side in the engine room.

"What's this all about, Tim?"

Before Tim could reply, the commander's voice came crackling over the loud-speaker again.

"Take her down!"

The boys shifted their body weight as they felt the nose of the submarine dip downward.

As the submarine plunged deeper and deeper toward the ocean floor, every man at his post increased his vigilance. The *Nautilus* was far below her cruising depth, a classified figure, known only to a few.

"Level off and stabilize!" The order was snapped out.

Not a person spoke. Only the faint sounds of the engines could be heard. Keen eyes scanned every part of the ship. Then, slowly, the tension decreased.

"What's this all about?" Steve repeated his question.

"We're in much colder water now," Tim replied. "You know how metal expands in heat and contracts in cold?"

"Sure," Steve answered.

"Well, this is a check. Sometimes a sub's fittings which are perfectly okay and tight in warm water, will start leaking if suddenly the water temperature drops. The metal contracts, you see."

"I get it."

Every compartment was checked, rechecked and checked again. Nothing was left to chance.

"Reporting to Diving Officer: All compartments report no leaks!"

A wave of relief swept through the *Nautilus*. It was almost physical. If any of the men had been asked about it, they would have answered: "You bet I felt it. I always feel good when I hear that report."

"Return to cruising depth," came the skipper's order. The *Nautilus'* elevator fins pointed her bow upward.

The *Nautilus'* speed was cut. In three days, the sub had come 1,700 miles from Seattle. Now, northward progress slowed. The sub had to thread its way through small islands in the shallow waters of the Bering Sea.

Not for one second were watchful eyes taken away from the fathometer.

Tim was on duty watching that all-important instrument on the afternoon watch of the third day. Steve, off duty, had wandered up to get the latest progress report. He stopped by his friend.

"Got plenty of water here, Tim?" he asked.

"I imagine the captain would like a lot more. We're barely crawling along here. Takes deep water for us to make any speed."

Tim recorded another figure taken from the fathometer.

*Not for one second were watchful eyes taken away from the fathometer*

"Remember how this thing works?" Tim asked.

"Sure, I guess so."

Tim, since the cruise had started, had spent more and more of his time studying the electronic operations on the *Nautilus*. Steve devoted most of his time to the nuclear propulsion machinery. Every man on the *Nautilus* had been trained in the use of all instruments and controls so that in an emergency, any member of the crew could take over any duty.

"It's the same kind of echo system that radar uses, isn't it?" Steve said.

"That's right. Only instead of being called 'radar,' it's called 'sonar,' " Tim said.

"I know, I know. I forget, though—how many feet per second does that signal travel?"

"Four thousand, eight hundred feet a second. That's the speed a sound signal travels to the bottom of the ocean and bounces back to the ship. So, multiply by seconds, or fractions of seconds, and we can tell just how deep the ocean is."

"Better than tossing a line overboard to measure with," Steve said, grinning.

"Yeah. And a lot dryer, too."

Suddenly Tim frowned. The fathometer showed the depth of the water beneath the *Nau*-

*tilus* to be decreasing rapidly. He made a quick report of the change. Commands were issued. The *Nautilus* slowed to a turtle crawl.

At the same time, word spread quickly through the sub.

"Ice! Ice! Dead ahead!"

The first serious ice had been picked up on the sub's electronic scanners. These were the sonar panels on the sub's bow which probed ahead of the craft for inverted ice peaks.

The *Nautilus* crept forward at reduced speed. Checks and reports of the water's depth were given every minute now. It seemed that the ice above and the ocean floor below were closing in.

A shiver of apprehension spread through the ship when it was reported that only twenty-five feet separated the top of the sub's sail from the under side of the ice above. And there was only forty-five feet of water between the sub's keel and the bottom of the ocean.

The *Nautilus* measures forty feet from sail top to keel. That means the sub was in a closing tunnel of one hundred feet of water.

Suddenly, the sub lurched as it went into a quick dive. The bow sonars had picked up a jagged dagger of ice extending thirty feet below the

*The sub was in a closing tunnel of one hundred feet of water*

surface. Now the *Nautilus* was being sandwiched in between top ice and ocean bottom.

There remained only twenty-five feet of clearance, top and bottom.

Captain Anderson held a hurried conference with his staff. A decision had to be made in seconds. To proceed was to risk wedging the *Nautilus* into an area between an upper crust of ice thirty feet thick and the bottom of the ocean.

Disappointment showed on the skipper's face. He knew what he had to do. He could not afford risking the safety of the crew and the magnificent submarine by trying to find a hole ahead to slip through.

He approached the Conning Officer.

"Reverse course," he ordered.

The western door, Radar's "back door," was closed.

# CHAPTER NINE

## Fortress of Ice

---

THE Nautilus made a wide-circle, sweeping turn and headed south. Every crewman knew the submarine was turning back. Every crewman fought back his disappointment and tried not to show it.

"Guess we're not going to make it," Steve said quietly to Tim.

Tim shrugged his shoulders.

"Must be tough on the skipper," Steve commented.

"What can he do?" Tim asked in reply. "You can't do the impossible, even in the *Nautilus*."

The two boys were quiet for a few minutes.

"Wonder where we're headed now? Steve said, half aloud. His answer came from the loudspeaker.

"This is the captain. The westward passage is

closed. We are going to try the eastern passage and the Alaskan route."

"Hey, how about that?" Steve's face lighted up.

"I knew the skipper wouldn't give up. We'll make it yet," Tim replied.

Spirits on the submarine bounced back up as rapidly as they had fallen. The crew went about its duties with restored confidence.

By the following morning, June 16th, the *Nautilus* had completed her withdrawal from the Siberian ice. She rounded the southern tip of St. Lawrence Island and again headed northward toward the Pole. Alaska was just east on the submarine's starboard side.

Tim, coming off the morning watch, awakened a sleepy Steve. Steve was due for the afternoon watch.

"We're heading for the Pole again, Steve," Tim said. "While you were knocking off your sack time, the captain announced we'd be running through shallow water and we'd have to cruise on the surface."

Steve groaned. "It *would* have to be on *my* watch!"

None of the crew liked being on duty when the submarine plowed along the surface. The going grew rougher as time went on. The sub was buffeted by four-foot waves dashing over the bow, sweeping the length of the ship and causing it to roll and pitch.

It was midafternoon, halfway through Steve's watch. The water was quite shallow, for a submarine. It was impossible for the *Nautilus* to duck under anything.

"Just like a prize fighter," one of the crewmen commented. "When you can't duck, you got to circle around."

And that's what the ship did. It zigged and zagged, dodging small ice flows. Progress toward the Pole remained at a turtle's pace.

Suddenly a cry came over the public address system that sent a chill of fear throughout the ship.

"Mast on the horizon! Dead ahead!"

The conning tower officer, Paul Early, spoke the words.

Captain Anderson rushed to the periscope. Every man came alert.

"Looks like a submarine to me," the skipper said, his eyes glued to the periscope.

The captain's words spread through the submarine like angry waters at the flood.

*"Looks like a submarine to me,"* the skipper said

"What's a submarine doing in these waters?"

"Might be a Russian sub."

The *Nautilus* was cruising with her sail partly out of water.

"If they sight us . . . well . . ."

In the torpedo room, men stared at one another. Their ears were strained for any command. The submariners formed a ring around the skipper, anxious to hear every word he spoke.

The silence became long, drawn out. Tension increased. Had they been spotted? If they had, what action could be taken? It was too shallow to submerge.

The *Nautilus* closed rapidly on the unknown object. Any moment now, a decision would have to be made.

Captain Anderson withdrew from the periscope. He turned to his waiting crew with a big smile on his face. "At ease, men. It's not a sub—only a big log—a tree trunk."

Everyone breathed easier. The backs of several hands brushed across foreheads, wiping off the sweat brought on by keyed-up nerves.

The tree trunk, with two upturned branches poking out of the water, looked exactly like a submarine with its two periscopes raised.

At this time, the *Nautilus* was off the mouth of the Yukon River. Logs and fallen trees had drifted down the Yukon and spread out over the sea. They became another obstacle to be dodged. Only an hour after sighting the first log, the *Nautilus* struck a log a glancing blow with its periscope. No damage was done.

Steve went off watch at 0400 hours and joined Tim in the Crew's Mess.

"Boy, oh boy! What a watch!"

"Yeah," Tim replied. "Heard you had a little excitement."

"A little! We had plenty. Where were you?"

"Having a good sleep."

"You always were lucky," Steve said.

At midnight, June 17th, the *Nautilus* drew nearer the restricted waters of the Bering Strait. Two islands guard the entrance to the Strait. One, Big Diomede, is owned by Russia. The other, Little Diomede, is American-owned. Powerful radar, both Russian and American, constantly scan the narrow gap between the islands.

For the *Nautilus* to be picked up on the radar scopes of either the Russians or its own country, might mean the end of the adventure. It would no longer be a secret that a nuclear-powered sub was approaching Arctic waters. Detection by the Russians could well bring on an international incident. If not, most certainly Russia would want to know why the *Nautilus* was in those waters.

Despite the shallow water, Captain Anderson ordered the submarine taken down to periscope depth. She was on a course between the two islands, heading for the Bering Strait. Only three feet of the slender, pipe-like periscope was exposed, cutting through the water like a snake's head ready to strike.

The *Nautilus* made it. She went through the Strait undetected and entered the Chukchi Sea. Four hundred miles across the Chukchi was the deep Arctic Basin. As one of the crewmen put it, if the submarine could reach the basin, then she had it made.

Once more, everyone on board was in high spirits.

"Well," said Radar, again taking over the conversation in the Crew's Mess. "It's like I always say. If they slam the back door in your face, go around to the front door."

Ice had closed the "back door," or western passage, but the front door was wide open.

The *Nautilus* kept zigging and zagging as she

encountered ice floes soon after entering the Chukchi Sea. The floes kept getting larger and larger. Shortly after nightfall, still running on the surface, the conning officer called the captain.

The sight ahead was a fearsome one. Under the cold, moonlit night sky, a barrier of ice rising up like a fortress blocked the *Nautilus* as far as the eye could see.

Even though the sub was still in shallow water, Captain Anderson gave the order to submerge. There was no way around this barrier of ice. The *Nautilus* would have to go under it.

Nerves tightened as the *Nautilus,* cruising at moderate speed, slid under the ice. A watchful crew tensed as suddenly the waters began to shoal rapidly and dangerously. Once more the sturdy craft was plunging into an ever narrowing wedge.

"We'll have to surface. See if we can find open water," the captain told the control officer.

The "ice pick" was ordered raised. This was the nickname given to the radio antenna. Captain Anderson kept the sub's periscope trained on the antenna as the *Nautilus* inched upward toward the surface. If the captain saw the "ice pick" start to bend, that would mean there was thick ice overhead. He'd have to "pull the cork" and submerge.

Luck was with the *Nautilus*. The "ice pick" stayed rigid, and the submarine surfaced in open water. She had come out on the other side of the wall of ice which had tried to block her passage.

There was little chance of detection in these remote, far reaches of the Chukchi Sea. Captain Anderson ordered all speed possible to make up for the time lost in the unsuccessful probe of the western door.

Ninety miles were logged in seven hours. Then, once more, the submarine was confronted with a horizon completely covered with towering ice. This barrier seemed endless. But this time, it was a welcome sight. It was felt that at long last, the *Nautilus* had finally reached the polar pack itself.

"Take her down," came the order.

The *Nautilus* crept under the ice. Everyone felt that the sub was entering on the last lap of her dangerous voyage. When next she surfaced and saw daylight and open water, she would be on the other side of the world, in Greenland.

Steve and Tim saw Captain Anderson speak to the conning officer, then turn and head for his stateroom. As he passed the boys, they could see how drawn his face had become. His eyes looked tired. His whole body showed the fatigue he felt from the long strain.

"Does he ever look tired!" Steve commented.

"You would be, too, if you hadn't had more than an hour or two of sleep a day for the past week," Tim said.

"I'd be asleep on my feet," Steve agreed.

The captain didn't get much sleep. Just one hour before noon on Tuesday, June 17th, he was awakened by the crackling of the control room officer's voice coming over the speaker in his stateroom:

"Captain, will you come in, please?"

The captain hurried to the control room.

"We just went under ice sixty-three feet thick. Our sail cleared it by only eight feet."

An order was snapped to the engine room.

"Back her off to dead slow."

The *Nautilus* was under a gigantic block of ice a mile wide, and not ten feet above the top of the sub's sail.

The submarine crept forward. Now the reports of the fathometer reading came in a steady chant. The bottom of the ocean was rising toward the sub's keel. Clearance overhead remained at eight feet. The sonar and other instruments told the captain that even worse conditions were just ahead.

Every man on board clenched his fists. No one

moved or spoke. The recording pen tracing the distance from the top of the sub's sail to the underside of the ice showed a bare five feet. Only five feet!

Any moment now, everyone expected to feel the shudder of the submarine as her topside ground against the ice above.

Then, suddenly, the gap widened. The *Nautilus* had scraped through.

But, relieved as he was, Captain Anderson's mind was still busy thinking of the electronic reports of what lay ahead.

There was only one thing to do: turn back.

## CHAPTER TEN

## *Top Secret T-Shirts*

HEADING south, the *Nautilus* plowed under-seas, retreating toward the Bering Strait. Gloom spread throughout the ship when the captain announced the second turn-back.

Was this the end of Operation Sunshine?

That was the unspoken question in the minds of every member of the submarine's crew.

The men were grim of face and sad of heart. There was no effort to conceal the disappointment which everyone felt. It showed all too plainly.

Shortly after the captain's announcement, Tim and Steve had taken to their bunks. Without speaking, both climbed in. They lay on their backs, each one staring sleeplessly at the bunk above. They, as well as the rest of the crew, shared their skipper's feelings. Operation Sunshine was a failure. That was all there was to it. It had been a noble try, but it hadn't come off.

In his closed stateroom, Captain Anderson sat at his desk. Painfully he wrote out the message to be radioed to the commander of naval operations in Washington.

The captain was a determined man. This message had to report the failure of the two polar probes. But Captain Anderson felt certain that the operation could still come off. In his message, he stated his firm belief that later in the summer, the attempt should be made again.

The crew knew nothing of this suggestion. The skipper could not tell them of it. He couldn't raise their hopes until he had heard from Washington and received his orders.

Captain Anderson knew that the heavy ice was still much farther south than had been expected at this time of the year. He also knew that within a few weeks, the ice would retreat as summer advanced. With the ice barrier farther north, in deeper waters, chances for the *Nautilus* to slip under the ice and make the passage would be greatly increased.

With this thought and this hope in mind, Captain Anderson ordered the submarine brought to the surface. The *Nautilus* made a vertical ascent —straight up. The skipper swung the periscope around. The skies were gray, the sea choppy, but there was no ice close enough to the submarine to interfere with it.

"All clear," he called out. "No close ice in sight. Raise the port whip. Radio, transmit the message to CNO."

The "port whip" was another radio antenna on the *Nautilus*. In moments, a Navy radio operator at Pearl Harbor flashed back, "I read you loud and clear." Captain Anderson's message went winging over the Pacific to Pearl Harbor, to be transmitted to Washington.

Sending the message seemed to clear away the gloom in the *Nautilus*.

"Well, that's that," was the general feeling on board. They had swung at their target and missed. Forget about it. What had happened was over and done with. No use griping about the past.

For the next few hours the *Nautilus* on her way south ran at periscope depth. The captain wanted to keep his port whip up to receive instructions

*Captain Anderson ordered the submarine brought
to the surface*

from Washington. The submarine couldn't receive messages when submerged.

After a few hours of running on the surface, the *Nautilus* was confronted with wide, thick barriers of ice. She had to submerge and run under the ice pack.

At midnight, the ship reached open water again. The captain ordered her to surface, and the radio whip was poked out of the water again to check for an answer from Washington. It came through right on the prearranged schedule for transmitting messages to the *Nautilus*.

CNO's message from Washington ordered the *Nautilus* to proceed to Pearl Harbor and wait for conditions to improve. The message ended:

"Set course and stand by for further instructions. Remain undetected."

The last two words of the message presented a problem.

Not only was the *Nautilus* to remain undetected, but that order meant that Operation Sunshine was to remain in the "Top Secret" security classification.

How was this to be done when 116 officers and men would be roaming around Hawaii for several weeks? Would it be possible for every one of these men to keep quiet about their recent adventure? And the possibility that they would try again?

There would be letters home. There would be meetings with crews of other submarines, meetings with former shipmates. Was it possible that no one would talk?

On June 20th, the *Nautilus* left the Bering Strait behind, with nothing but open water for the trip to Pearl Harbor. The cruise would be routine, with the one great big exception—a strictly enforced program to keep Operation Sunshine top secret.

The entire crew was assembled in the Crew's Mess. The captain spoke. From the seriousness in his expression and voice, the crew knew that if just one man spoke of the trip, any further attempt by the *Nautilus* to execute Operation Sunshine would be seriously jeopardized.

No one, the captain stressed, was to discuss any part of the operation. There was to be no communication, either by word of mouth or in writing either on board the submarine or on shore, with anyone.

"In other words," Tim said to Steve when the assembly had been dismissed, "we're to keep our big mouths shut."

"Yeah. Just a bunch of clams—that's us. Jeepers, I can't even talk about it to you."

"That's right."

Every man on board was ordered to go through his personal belongings and take out anything—letters, notes, diaries, charts—anything that had any relation to the recent voyage. Anything to be saved was to be put in envelopes labeled "Top Secret" and locked up in the submarine's safe.

"Here I've got a three-page letter all written telling Mom and Dad all about the cruise," Tim said to Steve.

"Tough, Tim. But you know what you got to do."

Tim did. He tore the letter into bits, shaking his head sadly. Writing a letter was a tough chore. But to have it all written, only to be forced to tear it up—that really hurt.

"Hey, what about these?" Steve held up two T-shirts. On their front, he had stenciled the North Pole insignia, designed by the ship's cartoonist. The insignia was to illustrate the submarine's transit of the North Pole.

"What am I going to do with these?" Steve exclaimed. "Jeepers, I don't want to have to lose them. I haven't got too many T-shirts."

"Come with me, my friend."

Tim led the way to the Crew's Mess. Steve followed right behind, clutching his telltale polar marked T-shirts. In the Mess, a petty officer was cramming various objects into a duffle bag with a Top Secret tag on it.

"Hand them over, Steve," Tim ordered.

The petty officer took the T-shirts. He looked them over carefully, then looked up at Steve with a big grin on his face.

"Sailor, you've just made history. This is the first time in the history of *any* navy that an undershirt has been classified as Top Secret."

Two days before reaching Pearl Harbor, the captain had a bulletin posted. This was the story to be used by the crew, a cover story to conceal the actual operation of the recent cruise. It was pure fiction and described an imaginary voyage toward the equator.

Early in the morning of June 28, the *Nautilus* was speeding underseas in the deep waters past Diamond Head, an extinct volcano and landmark of Hawaii. The captain had the course changed to steer southwest of the entrance to Pearl Harbor. Then he had the ship turned north. This way, when the *Nautilus* surfaced, she would appear to

be coming from the direction of the equator.

Not a single detail was omitted to keep Operation Sunshine still top secret.

# CHAPTER ELEVEN

## Four Weeks in Paradise

EXACTLY on schedule, the *Nautilus* slipped into Pearl Harbor on the morning of June 28th. A small boat came alongside, and two admirals boarded the submarine.

Hawaii gave the *Nautilus* an "aloha" that every member of the crew would remember for the rest of his life. In the inner harbor, another boat came alongside and draped a thirty-foot long lei of flowers over the sub's bows. Helicopters hovered overhead, dropping thousands of orchids on the surfaced underseas ship.

Blasts from the whistles of every tugboat and ship in the harbor shook the warm air. Fireboats shot plumelike sprays of water toward the sky. Thousands of people lined the shore and crowded the docks to see the arrival of the first nuclear-powered submarine.

Tim and Steve and others of the crew, spick and span in their navy "whites," rode the deck as the *Nautilus* approached its mooring.

On the dock a group of native girls danced a welcoming hula to the music of a navy band.

"Isn't this something?" Steve said to Tim. "Only way this reception could be any better would be if those fireboats were shooting up colored water!"

At 1000 hours, ten in the morning, the *Nautilus* was moored at the U. S. Submarine base in Pearl Harbor. Four hours later, a huge Navy transport plane took off with Captain Anderson and several other members of the *Nautilus* bound for Washington.

Captain Anderson had received orders while enroute to Pearl Harbor to report to the Pentagon in Washington. He would brief Navy officials there, and discuss the possibility of another try for the Pole later in the summer.

The skipper, a thoughtful, considerate man, had requested permission to bring other members of the crew along so they could pay a quick visit to their families. The captain selected only married officers and crewmen to make the trip.

On their return, only six days later, one of the lucky crewmen who had made the trip remarked: "Captain, that's the first time I've flown eleven thousand miles for a seventy-two hour liberty."

The *Nautilus* logged another first on her call to Pearl Harbor. This was the first time a nuclear-powered submarine had ever visited Hawaii. It seemed everyone on the island of Oahu wanted to visit the submarine. In the less than four weeks she lay at her Sierra One mooring, more than three thousand persons took guided tours of the sub. Another two hundred top naval personnel were taken on short cruises on the sub.

It was a busy time for every man on board—not only to take care of the visitors and answer hundreds of questions, but also because the captain had come back from Washington with good news. The *Nautilus* was to make another try at crossing from the Pacific to the Atlantic by way of the North Pole. This meant stepped-up activity to get the ship ready for her next try.

There wasn't much time left. Summer was drawing to its end.

Tim and Steve had looked forward to their call at Hawaii. There were so many things they wanted to see and do. They wanted to visit Diamond Head and Waikiki Beach. They wanted to try riding the surf. But there just wasn't time. Too much to do.

They did have shore leave the first Sunday in Hawaii. They were walking along a downtown street, taking in the sights, so different from anything they had ever seen before.

"Wish I was back in New London with the others," Tim said.

"Me, too. Gee, those guys are sure lucky.

Wonder what they're doing right now? Home with their families. Having fun. Wish I could have gone along."

"Sure, Steve. So do I. But you've got to admit it was only fair for the captain to take with him men who are married and have families."

"I know. I know. But I'd sure like to see my family right now," Steve sighed.

The boys walked along in silence for a block, both deep in their own thoughts. At a corner drugstore, Tim stopped and took Steve by the arm.

"How much money do you have with you?" Tim asked.

"I don't know. Not much. Why?"

"Well, see. Take a look. I've got an idea."

Steve dug into his pocket. He came up with

some change and a few bills. He counted the money slowly, carefully.

"Exactly nine dollars and twenty-three cents.

And that's got to last me until next pay day. How long before we get paid again?"

"About two weeks," Tim said absently. He was counting his money too.

"So what's this idea of yours?"

"I've only got a little over seven dollars," Tim said, more to himself than to Steve.

"The idea? The idea you said you had. What gives, Tim?"

"I was just thinking. How about us calling our families?"

"All the way from here to New London, Connecticut! You crazy or something? Man, that would cost a fortune."

"Oh, I don't know. We could find out."

"How?"

"Ask the operator. Come on. That is, if you like the idea."

"Like it! I think it's a swell idea. But it's going to cost, though."

"What else you going to do with your money? Buy a pineapple ranch?"

"Where would we call? Your house or mine?" Steve wanted to know.

"Now you got me. Where would they be this Sunday? Whose house?"

It had been the custom for many years for the Bordens to spend one Sunday afternoon and evening at the Kraniks', then the next Sunday the Kraniks spent the afternoon at the Bordens'.

"We could put the call in to my house, and if there's no answer, we could switch it to yours." Steve said.

"Now you're using the old brain, Stevie."

They were inside the drugstore. Tim entered the telephone booth. He talked several minutes. Steve could see Tim's mouth moving, but couldn't hear what he was saying.

Tim came out of the booth, a frown on his face.

"Well, how much?"

"Plenty. I wrote it down. This is Sunday, so rates are lower. Lower? Boy, they're still plenty high for a coupla near-broke sailors."

"So enough speech-making. How much?"

"For three minutes—that's station to station—it costs six dollars and seventy-five cents."

"That's not so bad," Steve said. "It would come to about three-fifty a piece."

"Sure, if we only talked three minutes. But there would be your mother and mine, our fathers, the kids and Cathy. We'd both have to talk to all of them. How long do you think that would take?"

"More than three minutes, that's for sure," Steve said. "How much for each extra minute over the first three?"

"Brace yourself, sailor, this is when it starts adding up—two great big fat dollars and one two-bit piece for each extra minute. In other words, $2.25 for each additional minute."

Steve let out a long, low whistle. "And we've got about sixteen bucks between us. Let me do some figuring."

Tim watched, a smile on his face, as Steve's brow became furrowed as he figured in his head.

"I'm counting on maybe ten minutes and we could talk to all of them. That would be $6.75 plus seven minutes overtime. Seven times $2.25—wow! That's over twenty bucks!"

"I know."

"And we haven't got that kind of money."

"Well, we could talk until our money ran out," Tim said. "You game for it?"

Steve was thinking. "I—I guess so."

"Okay, I'll put the call in." Tim reentered the booth.

Steve, standing outside, was still deep in thought. He saw Tim dial the operator, then saw his lips move. Steve frowned, shook his head, and pounded on the booth. Tim cracked the door, the receiver still at his ear.

"Yeah? Now what?"

"Cancel the call, Tim. I don't want to be broke all the time we're in Hawaii."

A look of disappointment came over Tim's face. Reluctantly he spoke to the operator and hung up.

The boys left the drugstore and walked in silence down the street.

Tim didn't like it a bit. He felt like giving Steve a piece of his mind. But he checked himself. He knew there was still a somewhat strained relationship between him and his friend. He also knew that he had been first to bring it on. He didn't see any point in opening the breech any wider.

The boys, their spirits down after they had been so high about making the call, called off their day in Honolulu and headed back for the Pearl Harbor submarine base.

Although Captain Anderson on his return made no formal announcement that he had been authorized to make a second attempt to execute Operation Sunshine, everyone on board sensed that he had. No one spoke about it, but everyone felt sure that the *Nautilus* would soon be North Pole bound again.

The submarine buzzed with activity. A television set was installed. Its transmitter was installed topside of the submarine facing up. This would give the crew a constant picture of the ice above. It would be of great help in spotting polynas, or leads—open pools of water in the ice— if it became necessary to surface. No longer would the sub have to creep upward inch by inch as an anxious crew wondered if the "ice pick" would bend or come out in open water.

Emergency breathing equipment for the entire crew was installed. About a third of the crew was already equipped. They had been ever since a smoky fire had broken out on their trip through the Panama Canal several weeks before. Now, if such an emergency should come up again, the entire crew would don masks and be able to breath despite acrid smoke and fumes.

The *Nautilus* made several trial runs to test the equipment. It worked fine with one objection. After one of the tests, Captain Anderson asked a crewman for his reaction to having to breathe for a long period through a mask.

"It's okay, Captain," he replied, "but it sure is a tough job to drink coffee with one of them on."

When the *Nautilus* was ready to set sail again

for its daring trip, a cover story was circulated that the submarine was to make a speed trial to Panama and would remain submerged the entire trip. It was still of the utmost importance that the sub's true destination remained a secret.

Not a word had been breathed about the unsuccessful trip. The captain paid tribute to his crew for the men's ability to keep the secret. For nearly four weeks the submarine and its crew of 116 men had been in Pearl Harbor. They had met and talked with thousands of persons. Not a single word of the sub's true mission had leaked out.

The morning of July 22nd found activity on board the submarine at its height. The last of the supplies were loaded aboard. Sacks of mail were handed down the hatches. It would be a long time before anyone on board would hear from home again.

As night approached, the captain gave the orders which put Operation Sunshine back in motion.

Lines were cast off. The *Nautilus* backed out of its slip.

She was on her way again.

# CHAPTER TWELVE

## *Mysterious Steve*

---

THE *Nautilus* was set on a due south course for her first miles out of Pearl Harbor. This was done to back up the cover story that she was on her way to the Panama Canal Zone.

With Hawaii ten miles behind her, the submarine changed course due east, ran that course until she was south and east of Diamond Head. Then she was pointed north.

Rounding Diamond Head in the darkness, the welcome words, "Mail Call," came over the loudspeakers.

There were letters for Tim and Steve, letters from their families. There was also a letter for Tim from Cathy. As he read it, a puzzled frown spread over his face. He read the paragraph again.

"It was too bad, Tim," Cathy wrote, "that you were on duty that Sunday when Steve called. We were all so disappointed that you couldn't be with him so we could talk to you, too."

What the dickens was going on here, Tim asked himself. Cathy must have been referring to the Sunday he and Steve were ashore and discussed telephoning their families. But it had been Steve who had decided not to make the call. Why, and when, had he put the call in? Tim thought back to that Sunday afternoon. He remembered they had returned to the submarine just in time for noon show. Afterward, they had played a few hands of cribbage. Then Steve had said he wanted to catch up on his sleep and had gone to his bunk.

Tim pressed his memory button. It came back to him. He remembered that he thought he had seen Steve slip through the Mess and head for the hatch. Checking a little later, Tim had found Steve's bunk empty.

Steve had gone back ashore, Tim concluded. He must have gone back ashore deliberately to make that long distance call. And most certainly, he hadn't wanted Tim to know about it.

At first, Tim thought he would ask Steve about it. Why had he been so secretive? "No way to treat a buddy," he thought angrily at first. Once he simmered down, Tim decided if Steve wanted to hold back on him, he must have a good reason.

"Anyway," Tim said to himself, half aloud, "He couldn't have talked very long. He only had nine bucks."

Tim shook his head. It was a puzzler, all right.

When the *Nautilus* had put Hawaii a safe distance behind, the captain once again ordered the identifying numbers 571 painted over. They had been painted back on the day before the submarine had arrived at Pearl Harbor.

The submarine's departure from Pearl Harbor was much different from its departure from Seattle. Then there had been happy excitement. The crew had been all keyed up at the prospect of the daring voyage. That same excitement no longer existed as the *Nautilus* headed north for its second try.

The men were old hands at polar probes by now. They went about their duties with a grim determination. They were veterans. They knew what lay ahead of them. This time they were going to see it through.

There was no lack of confidence. But neither was there the over-optimism that had marked their first attempt.

The charts in the control room showed that on this trip, the *Nautilus* was going to go through the "back door," the western passage. Reports had shown that this passage was free of ice. The western route was shorter, and Captain Anderson wanted to attempt the passage under the Pole as quickly as possible.

The *Nautilus* was running submerged at full speed. Its reactor was called upon for every ounce of power. The submarine was on automatic pilot, aimed directly at the Bering Strait, and darting toward it as straight as an arrow.

At eight o'clock that night, the captain's voice came over the loud-speaker system.

"All hands. The *Nautilus* has just logged her 120,000th mile under the sea. That's 40,000 leagues, exactly twice the 20,000 leagues under the sea logged in Jules Verne's book of the same name. That is all."

"I read that book," Steve said excitedly. "When we were in boot camp. Imagine—we've gone twice as far. And nobody ever believed that what Jules Verne wrote would ever come true."

Tim only smiled in reply.

Twenty-four hours out of Pearl Harbor, the *Nautilus* came up to periscope depth and poked her radio whip out of the water.

The report from Pearl was a good one. Ice conditions in the Chukchi Sea had greatly improved.

Spirits and enthusiasm rose when this report circulated throughout the ship. Confidence grew.

"We'll make it this time," a crewman muttered. Others nodded their heads in agreement.

On the morning of the seventh day out of Pearl Harbor, the *Nautilus* was aimed for the narrow slot forming the Bering Strait. She shot the slot at full speed and was once more back in the Chukchi Sea.

This time, though, instead of being confronted with massive floes of ice, the sea was clear. No need for zigging and zagging. The *Nautilus* sped across the forty miles of shallow, shoal water in hours. On the first trip, it had taken over a full day to thread through the ice-covered stretch.

At midnight of the same day, seven days out of Pearl Harbor, the *Nautilus* reached a point sixty miles farther north than she had reached on her first attempt.

Through the periscope, Captain Anderson could see huge chunks of ice. The submarine skirted these floes, searching for the true polar pack.

From what he saw, Captain Anderson knew that even though conditions were greatly improved over the first probe, the trip was not going to be an easy one. He described the ice as "mean-looking, dirty, ragged, zagged, highly ridged, and hummocked."

Would he be forced to turn back again? The captain strode toward his stateroom. Silent crewmen stared at his thoughtful face as he passed them. Then, with questioning looks on their faces, the crew stared at one another.

# CHAPTER THIRTEEN

## *"Let's Go! Go! Go!"*

---

Radar, the crewman with the big ears, Tim and Steve, along with other crewmen were in the Crew's Mess. They were off duty, and ordinarily would have been sleeping. But this was no ordinary time. Nobody could sleep for long as the *Nautilus* moved swiftly under water toward her first goal—the North Pole.

Conversation moved in quick starts and quicker stops. Everyone would be either talking at once or suddenly silent. "Shooting the breeze," the sailor's phrase for just talking, was becoming more difficult. Only one thought was foremost in the minds of everyone aboard:

"Will we make it this time?"

Everyone who had seen the captain's drawn, tired face, knew that he, too, had the same thought in his mind.

Steve stretched, yawned, and said, "Think I'll try to catch some shut-eye. Good time for it now. Can't tell when we'll have another chance." He got up and headed for his bunk.

About ten minutes later, Tim decided to do the same. His bunk was directly opposite Steve's. Tim started to fold himself into his bunk. He looked over at Steve. Steve was wide awake, unblinking eyes staring upward.

"Steve?"

Steve grunted a "Hunnhh?" in reply without stirring.

"I'd like to talk to you for a minute."

"About what?"

"About you and me. What's happened to us?"

Steve didn't answer.

"I mean—well, it seems to me that for the past month or so, well, we don't seem to be as buddy-buddy as we used to be. I mean, I think you're holding something back from me."

"And how about you?" was Steve's comeback. "You started the whole thing."

"What do you mean, *I* started it?"

*Everyone who had seen the captain's drawn, tired face knew that he, too, had the same thought*

Steve turned over on his side, propping up his head on his hand.

"Look, Tim, remember that day when we went out and got that 'Stop Leak' stuff?"

"Sure. Of course I remember it."

"And that night? We had extra shore leave. I asked you to go to the movies with me. But oh, no, not you. You had something else to do. You gave me a fast brush-off. You practically told me to mind my own business."

Tim didn't reply at once. Steve, he knew, was right. It had been his, Tim's, doing at the start. There was something he was holding back from his friend. Over and over he had wrestled with his conscience. The result had always come out the same. Tim felt he couldn't tell Steve. It would hurt him too much. Should he tell him now? Or should he wait until the cruise was over? It would be over in another ten days if all went well. Tim decided to hold back a little longer.

It crossed Tim's mind, though, that Steve had some explaining to do, too. What about that telephone call Cathy had referred to in her letter?

"I have to go along with you, Steve. I guess I was sort of short with you, even rude, that night. But I had a reason for not going with you."

"So, that's all I wanted to know—what the reason was. I still would like to know."

Tim decided to take the tactic that a good offense is better than a good defense. Instead of answering Steve's question, he shot a question at him.

"I got a letter from Cathy the day we left Pearl Harbor. She told me you *did* call home that Sunday. How come you slipped ashore and made the call without me? It was my idea in the first place, remember."

"Yeah. I know," Steve replied. For several moments he was silent. "Okay, Tim. I did go back ashore. I did made that call. I didn't like keeping it from you. But it was a real personal thing. Oh, you'll find out about it soon enough. But I'm still sort of mixed up—don't know yet just what I'm going to do . . ."

"What do you mean, you don't know what you're going to do?"

"It's something I may have to do," Steve answered.

"Like what?"

"Like get out of the Navy."

Tim stepped across the narrow aisle and grabbed Steve by the shoulders.

"Get out of the Navy! What do you mean? You can't get out of the Navy! That's crazy! Why . . . why . . . all your life . . ."

Steve just looked up at him.

"Now look, Steve, you've got to tell me about it. Why, Steve? Why are you talking like this?"

Silently, Steve looked at his friend. Tim's face was furrowed with concern. Steve made up his mind. Perhaps telling Tim about the whole thing would help both of them.

"It's like this, Tim. I got a letter just as we left that first time from Seattle. The letter was from Cathy. I knew that what she told me would worry you, almost as much as it worries me. So, since we were just setting out on this big deal, this trip under the Pole, I thought I'd wait before telling you. I also wanted time to figure it out for myself. I mean, what I had to do."

"It must really be something, Steve, for you to think about getting out of the Navy. I know how badly you want to make the Navy your career."

"I sure do, Tim. But . . . I don't think I'm going to be able to."

"Can you tell me why, now? Maybe we both better come clean. You tell me your reason. I tell you mine."

[ 137 ]

The two boys, once more close friends, the atmosphere of suspicion between them clearing, shook hands.

"It's like this—"

"It's like this—"

Both spoke together. Then they laughed.

Before they could go on, they felt the submarine tilt. Her bow was slanting upward. The *Nautilus* was planing toward the surface.

"All hands! . . . All hands! . . ."

"Jeepers! I wonder what's up?" Steve leaped out of his bunk. Tim was already on his way to the Crew's Mess.

The ship had come to a stop by the time the boys reached the Mess. The *Nautilus* had planed to within fifty feet of the surface, and now the skipper had ordered her taken up in a vertical ascent.

The television screen showed only blocks of ice above. They were big blocks, but not a solid covering of ice. But the captain didn't want to risk damage to the sub's periscopes by coming up too fast and banging into one of those floating ice blocks.

The submarine surfaced. The captain noticed that in surfacing, the *Nautilus* had trapped a small piece of ice on its deck. He smiled. An idea had flashed through his mind. He turned to the men standing around him, all of them staring at him with wide, questioning eyes.

"You, Kranik, and you, Borden . . . Smith, Miller. The four of you. Up the hatch and bring me back that hunk of ice."

The four men named looked at each other in astonishment. Just what did he want with a hunk of polar ice? But what the captain ordered, the captain got.

Up the hatchway they went. The hunk of ice was retrieved, and handed down below. When the four icetrappers were back below, the captain explained.

"Put that piece of ice in the deep freeze. I think it might make a nice souvenir for Admiral Rickover." He smiled and strode away toward his stateroom.

Admiral H. G. Rickover, father of the atomic-powered submarine, did appreciate the hunk of polar ice. It wasn't presented to him for several weeks, of course, but when he did receive it, he indicated that no one other thing brought from North Pole waters could have given him any greater pleasure.

*The hunk of ice was retrieved and handed below*

The *Nautilus* plunged under the seas again. She nudged along the edge of the ice pack. The fathometer kept pinging for deep water. Every probe ended in a dead end. Time and time again the skipper ordered a course only to find it closed after a short under-water run.

Time was running out. Captain Anderson knew that in Washington, top-level officials were anxiously awaiting news of the submarine's progress.

Progress was slow. The hours sped by, but still the long-looked-for deep water channel under the ice eluded the *Nautilus* and her crew.

A feeling of gloom and desperation filled the craft. The skipper ordered a complete change in course and headed east toward the Barrow Sea Valley.

With this change of course, there were many whispered conferences among the crew.

"Are we licked again?"

"We didn't make it on that course on our first probe."

The submarine ran along the boundary of the ice pack. Long arms of rugged ice, blown down from the pack by a north wind, blocked the sub's path with disheartening frequency. Once the submarine was caught between two of these long ice arms and was forced to reverse course.

Just north of Point Franklin, Alaska, when the hopes of all had reached their lowest level, quick sweeps by the submarine's radars showed she had rounded the corner of the pack. At long last, the *Nautilus* was headed for the Barrow Sea Valley. This was the deep-water gateway to the Arctic Basin.

As the *Nautilus* planed below the surface, Captain Anderson took a final look through the periscope. He saw a full moon setting and a blazingly bright sun rising.

"This is it," he said to himself. "Let's go, go, go!"

# CHAPTER FOURTEEN

## *Nearing the North Pole*

---

CAPTAIN ANDERSON'S rising spirits and his new feeling of optimism soon spread throughout the ship. Worried faces gave way to smiling ones. Some of the crew made the V for victory sign. Others, although feeling confident, kept their fingers crossed.

The fathometer showed the ocean's valley floor growing deeper and wider. The *Nautilus* was taken down deep, and an eighteen-knot speed was ordered. She was running under the true polar pack.

The polar pack is a solid mass of ice extending in a two-thousand-mile-wide circle with the North Pole in the circle's center. It was under this tremendous mass of ice that the *Nautilus* would travel, if the water were deep enough. Once under it, heading north, then east for the exit into the Greenland Sea, the submarine would be unable to surface.

The skipper spoke to the helmsman.

"Come left to north."

Dead ahead, 1,094 miles away was the North Pole.

Eight hundred miles beyond the pole was the edge of the pack where the *Nautilus* would be able to surface. If all went well, the submarine would make the first crossing from the Pacific to the Atlantic Ocean, pioneering a new northwest passage.

This was the submarine's primary mission. Reaching the North Pole, of course, would make history. But the importance of the cruise was to determine if such a northwest passage was practical.

With the sub's powerful reactor operating smoothly, with every instrument on its best behavior, the feeling among the crew was, "We're home free."

They weren't. And of all things to get out of whack and endanger the success of the expedition, it was the submarine's garbage disposal unit.

At first the failure of this necessary unit was amusing to the crew.

"Just like at home, Steve," Tim said. "Remember, coupla summers ago?"

"I sure do. What a mess!"

Tim laughed. "Dad had just had a disposal installed. Then the thing jammed the first week we had it."

"But we fixed it," Steve said.

"But it was some job, clearing out all the gunk that had got trapped inside."

On the *Nautilus,* the garbage disposal unit (GDU) is a ten-inch tube that runs from the scullery down through the bottom of the sub. It works very much like a torpedo tube. There are two trap doors, an outer door and an inner one. With the outer door closed, bags of refuse are slipped into the tube. Once they're at the bottom, the inner trap door is closed. Then the tube is pumped full of water. The pressure opens the outer door, letting the refuse bags slide safely into the sea.

Now the GDU was clogged. It was no minor problem either. There were 116 men on board the *Nautilus.* That meant 348 meals a day. There were a lot of leavings from that many meals. They had to be gotten rid of.

The Damage Control Officer formed an emergency task force for Operation Clean-up. Using the sub's emergency air system, they forced air into the tube until the air pressure inside was greater than the water pressure outside. If this had not been done, water would have come rushing inside the sub as they dislodged the two jammed garbage bags, stuck in the outer door. The garbage task force used long poles, and finally the system was cleaned up.

"Heck," Steve joked when the job was done.

"Back home, my mother sometimes has as much trouble getting me to take the garbage out."

With each hour the distance between the *Nautilus* and the Pole was shortened. She was running at eighteen knots. The captain ordered her brought up to twenty knots.

Steve and Tim were having coffee.

"This is the life, Steve," Tim said. "If you've got to explore the North Pole—this is the way to do it. A warm ship, hot food—all the comforts of home."

"It sure beats doing it on the surface. I was just reading what Admiral Peary said about that polar pack upstairs. Got the book right here." Steve flipped over a few pages. "Listen: he says, 'The polar pack near the North Pole is a trackless, colorless chaos of broken and heaved-up ice.' How'd you like to be walking across that heaved-up ice?"

"Not for me, Steve. I never did like it too cold. I've just promised myself that on all my trips to the North Pole, I'm going by submarine."

On Saturday morning, August 2, just twelve days out of Pearl Harbor, the *Nautilus* was cruising at a depth of four hundred feet. She was aimed directly at the North Pole. It had been figured out that if the sub could hold her present course and run at the same speed, she would hit the North Pole in forty-four hours.

There was plenty of water underneath the sub's keel. And there was plenty of ice overhead. The ice was rough and solid, projecting downward sixty-five feet from the surface.

With their goal in sight, the captain and his executive officer stood "watch and watch." One of the two officers was up and directing the submarine's operations at all times. Neither man had more than a fast two hours of sleep at any one time.

The *Nautilus* continued her steady, swift progress northward. Again, as on the first trip, everyone on board tightened up as the ship neared its goal.

Excitement grew to a burning high. Morale was never better.

Onward went the *Nautilus.*

Every instrument was under constant observation. Men grouped under the television set, scanning the jagged ice peaks overhead, peaks that looked like daggers ready to plunge into the ship's topside.

Would they make it? If not, where was the point of no return? Was it miles away? A hundred miles? At the North Pole itself?

*Men grouped under the television set*

At one point, ice peaks extending 125 feet below the surface were spotted.

Reports from fathometer readings came in a steady, monotonous report.

The submarine was running smoothly, swiftly on its course. It seemed that only an equipment failure could halt the sub's northward surge now. Instruments were checked constantly. Vigilance increased.

The captain came to the fathometer and relieved the crewman on duty. He stayed by it for several hours. The readings told him of steep, undersea cliffs, undersea mountain ranges, some of them rising thousands of feet from the ocean's floor.

There was plenty of water beneath the good ship. At times the fathometer registered depths of 1,500 fathoms—9,000 feet. Once, the fathometer peaked up to 500 fathoms, still 3,000 feet of water, but the captain felt relieved when again the instrument showed greater depth.

The skipper wandered from instrument to instrument. He made an endless tour of the craft. In the engine room, he spoke briefly to the officer in charge and nodded to Steve and Tim. Only Tim was on duty, but Steve had joined him—

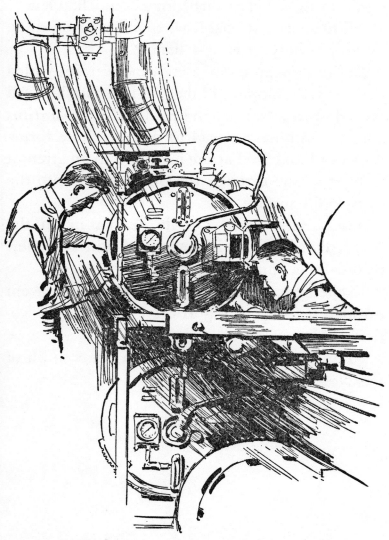

*Only Tim was on duty, but Steve had joined him*

ready to help out if anything should happen.

All the men on board, whether on or off duty, stood by ready to lend a hand.

In the torpedo room, a crewman carefully bled just the right amount of oxygen into the ship. All torpedo tubes were at the ready. If the *Nautilus* got into trouble and had to surface, those torpedoes would be fired at the ice above in an attempt to blast a hole through the thick covering so the ship could surface.

The *Nautilus* was rapidly closing in on the North Pole. Each mile northward now set a new record for a ship of any type.

Excitement reached new heights and swept through the ship. A report came from the navigation officer.

"The *Nautilus* is now only two hours south of the North Pole!"

# CHAPTER FIFTEEN

## *Right on the Nose*

---

ONE hour to go . . . thirty minutes . . . fifteen.

Now was the time when every man on the *Nautilus* was sweating it out. The captain, the navigator, and a petty officer were stationed in the attack center.

The ice above was varying in thickness from eight to eighty feet. The thinner spots were carefully plotted on the charts—just in case torpedoes had to blast a hole in the ice for the submarine to surface.

Half-degree adjustments were made at the helm. The captain was determined to hit the North Pole right on the nose. Position indicators were checked each minute.

The electronic log—the sub's speedometer—showed the ship holding steady at twenty knots. The depth gauge needle showed the ship to be running at four hundred feet beneath the surface. Soundings showed that the ocean depth was eight thousand feet.

It was August 3rd. The *Nautilus* had been under ice for sixty-two hours.

One mile south of the Pole. The captain spoke to Navigator Jenks.

"Tell me when we're four-tenths of a mile away."

Jenks nodded his head.

The Crew's Mess and the Attack Center were crowded with breathless, speechless members of the crew.

"Electronic log reads four-tenths away, Captain."

Commander Anderson stepped to the mike of the ship's public address system.

"All hands . . . this is the Captain speaking . . . In a few moments, *Nautilus* will realize a goal long a dream of mankind—the attainment by ship of the North Geographic Pole. With continued Godspeed, in less than two days we will record an even more significant historic first: the completion of a rapid transpolar voyage from the Pacific to the Atlantic Ocean.

"The distance to the Pole is now precisely four-tenths of a mile. As we approach, let us pause in silence dedicated with our thanks for the blessings that have been ours during this remarkable voyage —our prayers for lasting world peace, and in solemn tribute to those who have preceded us, whether in victory or defeat."

The captain's voice was the only human sound in the ship. The only other sound was the steady pinging from the sonars as they probed the bottom, the ice and the dark waters dead ahead.

The juke box was shut off.

The distance indicator showed that the nose of the *Nautilus* was seconds away from the Pole. The captain began his countdown to the crew.

"Stand by. 10 . . . 8 . . . 6 . . . 4 . . . 3 . . . 2 . . . 1. MARK! August 3, 1958. Time, 2315 (11:15 Eastern Daylight Saving Time). For the United States and the United States Navy, the North Pole!"

Cheers burst out from all hands. They shook the ship, rattled plates, cups, and pans in the galley.

The skipper looked at the navigator.

*They rattled plates, cups, and pans in the galley*

"Did we hit it on the nose?" he asked.

"As a matter of fact, Captain," came the reply, "you might say we came so close we pierced the Pole."

# CHAPTER SIXTEEN

## *"Nautilus 90 North"*

---

Out! Out, small fry!"

Tim and Steve had poked their heads into the galley where Commissaryman Jack Baird was engaged in a delicate piece of work. He pointed a pastry "gun" filled with frosting menacingly at them.

"Can't you see there's an artist at work?" Baird was putting the finishing touches on a huge slab of cake. On the top, he had drawn in frosting the *Nautilus'* polar flag. Carefully, he traced the head of the arrow which marked the submarine's course.

"Walt Disney could use you," Tim said, grinning as he ducked back into the passageway leading to the Crew's Mess.

A party spirit had the run of the ship. This time there was something big to celebrate. Choice steaks and the special cake were on the menu for this gala day.

Electrician's Mate First Class James Sordelet came up behind the boys and elbowed his way through them. "Going to make a little history on my own. Come on in and see."

Steve and Tim crowded into the mess room. "What's George Washington think he's going to do?" Steve whispered to Tim.

The two boys looked on as Sordelet stepped forward and raised his right hand. They listened as he spoke in firm tones.

"I'll be darned!" Tim said, awestruck. "He *did* make history. He's the first sailor in history to reenlist at the North Pole!"

"Brace yourself for our own little ceremony," Steve murmured to Tim.

Now, eleven men stepped forward. Among them, standing proudly erect, were Tim Borden and Steve Kranik. These men, after hour upon hour of off-duty study, making drawings, checking pipes, switches, valves, had passed stiff examinations. Here was their reward:

"By your hard work, your keen interest, and

your desire to advance yourselves, you have successfully passed your examinations and are now qualified in nuclear submarines."

Another cheer went up as the United States Navy added eleven more men to its growing number of submariners capable of serving aboard the newest naval arm, atomic-powered underseas ships.

Tim and Steve turned to one another and shook hands. "Wow," they said both at once.

"And you can add a 'whew' to that," Steve said. "I didn't think I was going to get through it."

Captain Anderson commanded the attention of all the men in the mess. The crew quieted down. The captain wanted his crew to share in the tribute to be paid to the man who, more than any other, had made the historic voyage possible. The man was President Dwight D. Eisenhower.

"I have written a letter to the President," the skipper explained, "thanking him for his backing and confidence that we could bring Operation Sunshine to a successful conclusion. I will read you the last sentence: 'I hope, sir, that you will accept this letter as a memento of a voyage of importance to the United States.'"

The captain signed the letter as the crew cheered.

Relaxing after the rather solemn and historic events, the men broke into laughter as a booming, "Ho-Ho-Ho" rang down the passageway. In burst Santa Claus. He was Bill McNally, jolly and red-faced from the vegetable coloring smeared over his face. His beard was a long length of medical cotton. His suit was made from red flagging material.

"What are you doing, dropping garbage all over my front lawn?" were his first words. "And what are you doing up here in my backyard when it's my busiest season?" he asked in mock anger. "Don't you know me and my elves are busy day and night getting ready for Christmas? Got a lot of toys to make. So, I'll thank you to get this submarine out of here so I can get back to work. Merry Christmas!"

Laughter and jokes continued as the men, their appetites increased by the relaxing fun, did away with steaks, all the "fixings," and the huge decorated cake.

Far above the *Nautilus,* the polar ice lay thick and heavy. The submarine sped along her east-

*In burst Santa Claus*

ward course at a smooth, even twenty knots.

Life on the submarine returned to normal. The juke box came back on. There was a line at the coffee urn. Some of the crew made for their bunks, needing sleep after so many hours of tense, keyed-up watchfulness as the sub had approached its first goal.

"Going to hit the sack, Tim?" Steve asked his friend.

"I sure am. But look at this first. Some figures the captain got up. Just been posted."

Steve looked at the figures Tim had copied.

"I'm going to put these in a letter. 'Member back in high school when we had that class debate about what would happen if the Panama Canal were closed? Figure it this way now. I mean, if the Canal were closed, we could *still* get from the Atlantic to the Pacific. And a lot faster, too, by coming under the pole."

"I see. Jeepers, look how much shorter the route from Japan to Europe is by way of the Pole— 4,900 miles shorter. Boy, when they build cargo subs, they can cut almost two weeks off the trip."

"Plenty of water for the biggest sub, too," Tim added, still reading from the figures he had copied. "Depth of the sea here is 13,410 feet. How about that?"

"Guess we made history, all right," Steve said.

"We sure did," Tim agreed. "All we have to do now is get to open water so we can tell the world about it."

"All this sailor's got to do right now," Steve said, "is to hit the sack. Boy, am I ever tired. You with me?"

Tim nodded. Briefly, a thought crossed his sleepy mind. "Steve and I still haven't talked out his problem." He decided this was no moment to discuss quitting the Navy. The boys headed for their bunks. In fifteen minutes they were both asleep.

There was no sleep for Captain Anderson. The *Nautilus* had truly carried off a tremendous feat. The first leg, and the longest one, of a submerged northwest passage had been charted. Reaching the North Pole in a submarine with 116 men aboard was—in itself—an accomplishment that would thrill the world. The big goal was still a big "if." If the submarine could complete its northwest passage, it would achieve the first transpolar trip from the Pacific Ocean to the Atlantic Ocean.

If all went well, open water would be reached in a day and a half.

The *Nautilus* continued on course, heading for the Greenland-Spitzbergen portal, the water doorway between those two islands into the Atlantic Ocean. Once through, the *Nautilus* would be aimed for Portland, England, the destination announced by the captain when the submarine left Seattle on her first probe.

Hour after hour the *Nautilus* ran under ice, seeking open water. The 116 men on board were still confident, but edgy.

In Washington, anxiety was increasing. The submarine had been unreported for several days. No word had come winging through the air that the Pole had been reached, that the submarine was on course, that it was heading for the open waters of the Atlantic.

Finding open water and getting a message off to the Chief of Naval Operations in Washington became more and more urgent.

Ninety-six hours had passed since the *Nautilus* had last been on the surface of the sea. How much longer would it be? Was the ship having compass trouble and running in wide circles still near the Pole? These were some of the many questions tumbling through the captain's head.

"Conning officer reporting." The words came

[ *166* ]

crackling over the loud-speakers. Everyone came to silent attention.

"We have just reached a patch of clear blue water."

Sighs of relief, like the sound of escaping steam, came from the nerved-up crewmen.

Tim looked at Steve, his broad smile matching the wide grin of his friend.

"Boy, will it ever be good to see daylight again!" Tim said.

"I'll buy all the daylight you can sell me," Steve agreed.

The skipper was at the periscope. He studied the blue-green water. Minutes passed. The crew on duty at the detection equipment flashed the good news.

"All clear overhead."

The ship stopped. Up went the whip antenna, the "ice-pick." No chances were going to be taken now. "All clear overhead" had been reported, but the captain didn't want to risk success at this point by surfacing and possibly bumping against a layer of clear ice.

The *Nautilus* inched upward.

The periscope broke surface. Brilliant sunlight poured into the glass.

"The sun always shines on the *Nautilus*," Tim cracked to Steve.

In the radio room, two men were frantically turning knobs and flipping switches. They needed every ounce of power they could build up to transmit the captain's world-shaking message.

Communications in the Arctic are always unreliable. Sometimes it takes hours to get a signal through. At other times, it is as easy as making a local telephone call.

Radioman Provost was repeating the same message time after time.

"Any U. S. Navy radio station! This is an unidentified station with two operational immediate messages."

No reply.

Provost pounded out the message on his telegraph key again.

Wouldn't some station come in? Here was the *Nautilus* bursting with news for the ears of the whole world. No one seemed to want to hear it.

"Guess we need some carrier pigeons," a crewman joked.

The captain was just about to submerge for a fast run south, to reach a position where transmission would improve when a faint signal came through.

"This is U. S. Navy radio, Japan."

Moments later, the captain's historic three-word message was on its way to Washington by way of Japan.

"Nautilus 90 North."

That was all. Just three words. But three words that would thrill the world. Three words that meant that the *Nautilus* reached the North Pole, had slid under it, and had now completed the first transpolar passage from the Pacific to the Atlantic.

Operation Sunshine had been completed with flying colors.

# CHAPTER SEVENTEEN

## *Homeward Bound*

---

THE *Nautilus* was a fast craft. But the events springing from her succesful trip moved even faster. Three days after the famous three-word message had been shot into the air from her "ice pick," the submarine lay just below the surface of the water off Reykjavik, Iceland.

This was a rendezvous point. The *Nautilus* was waiting, lying hidden from other shipping until her radar picked up the blip that would mean a helicopter was nearing the sub.

Eyes scanned the radar screen.

"There she is!" came a shout as a blimp appeared.

"Take her up!" the conning officer ordered.

The *Nautilus* rose to periscope depth. As the "chopper" came into the periscope's field, the captain ordered three blasts on the surfacing alarm, and the submarine broke the water as she came to the surface.

The bridge hatch cleared the water. Captain Anderson climbed up the hatchway, followed by members of his crew.

The helicopter hovered directly overhead. In seconds the captain's gear was hoisted aboard the 'copter. His hands grasped the rung of the rope ladder hanging down from the plane.

"Watch it, Captain," Tim said, giving the captain a boost. "That's a big step you're taking."

Captain Anderson scrambled inside the cockpit. Men on the *Nautilus* stood at attention. The captain's hand snaked out, holding a white envelope. Tim took it. The 'copter rose slowly into the air, dipped, then headed for Iceland.

"See you in Merrie Olde England," Tim shouted.

In minutes, the helicopter was out of sight. In fifteen minutes it would land in Greenland. Captain Anderson would transfer to a fast Navy transport and be flown to Washington.

He would be taken directly to the White House. There, and with the smiling President of the United States facing a battery of newspapermen, the world would hear of the fantastic journey of the U. S. S. *Nautilus*—a real-life trip which made the "20,000 Leagues Under the Sea" of the fictional *Nautilus* only a trial run.

Back inside the *Nautilus*, Tim handed the envelope he had taken from Captain Anderson to Frank Adams, the sub's Executive Officer. Adams would be in command of the ship until Captain Anderson rejoined her off Portland, England.

The group surrounding Adams was silent as he tore open the envelope. He stepped quickly to a microphone. This was something he wanted the whole crew to hear.

"Now hear this. All hands! All hands!" Then, his voice filled with emotion, he read: " 'To the officers and crew of the *Nautilus*: Congratulations on the magnificent achievement—WELL DONE.' " Adams paused, then added, "that message is signed, 'Dwight D. Eisenhower.' "

Five days later the *Nautilus* lay motionless on the surface of Atlantic Ocean waters just off Portland, England. She was awaiting the return of her skipper, Commander William R. Anderson. He had crossed on a Navy transport and was to be

*"Now hear this. All hands! All hands!"*

flown out in a helicopter to resume command of his famous submarine.

Tim and Steve were huddled in a corner of the Crew's Mess.

"Okay now, Steve, give out. We'll be going home soon. Let's clear the air about what's been bothering both of us during this voyage."

Steve frowned. He took a deep breath, and let his shoulders slump forward. He looked so down, so unhappy, that Tim felt he had better talk first.

"Look, Steve. I don't know about you, but I— well, what I've been keeping back from you may come as a surprise, but I guess you won't hate me too much for it."

"You know I could never hate you, Tim."

"That night, back in Seattle when you asked me to go to the movies with you and I gave you the brush-off—I had a big date—not the kind you're thinking of—I had an appointment with the exec. officer."

Tim paused. Steve raised his head and looked at his friend with curious interest.

"Only the day before, I had taken a top test in an electronic program. I really hit. Scored better than I dared hope. So, after that, the exec. asked me if I'd ever thought about becoming an officer."

Tim paused again to see what effect this would have on Steve.

"I hadn't until then," Tim continued, "but it surely got me excited. That night, see, the exec. had arranged to tell me all about it. What I'd have to do. What I'd have to study. That's why I couldn't go with you."

"But what made you feel you couldn't tell me about it?" Steve asked.

"I really don't know, for sure," Tim said, shrugging his shoulders. "I guess I just felt that if you knew I was going to try to make officer, go to Officer's Candidate school, you might think I was getting—you know—swell-headed or something. We'd always planned to be shipmates. I thought you might resent the whole thing."

Steve didn't answer for a moment. Then he rose to his feet and whacked Tim on the back. He grabbed him by the shoulders, pulled him from his chair, and waltzed him around.

"Make any difference! You're out of your ever-lovin' mind! I think that's the greatest. I'm *proud* of you."

The boys sat down again. Tim was beaming foolishly at his friend's praise.

"Really, Tim, I couldn't be happier," Steve

[ *175* ]

said earnestly. "And you'll make it, too. I know that for real, *real* sure."

After a silence, Steve spoke again. "I envy you, Tim. I had hopes of doing the same. In nuclear propulsion, though, not electronics like you."

"Then why don't you try for it?" Tim said eagerly. "You've learned a lot. You've qualified—and under the North Pole, yet. You're getting to be a top man on this sub. I know you could make it."

Steve shook his head. "Maybe so, but I have my doubts. Anyway, I'm never going to get the chance."

"Why not? Look, have you spoken to the exec.?"

"No. And I'm not going to, Tim," Steve stared seriously at Tim. "I'm going to have to get released from the Navy."

"Quit the Navy?" Tim was astounded.

"Yes, Steve. I don't want to. You know that. But I got a letter from Cathy. I confirmed what I was most afraid of when I made that telephone call from Honolulu. Cathy had written me that my dad had had a heart attack. Oh, she said it was a mild one. She tried to keep me from being worried. But I couldn't help worrying. That's why I made that call without you. I didn't want you to know about it. Mostly I guess because I didn't know what I was going to do—going to *have* to do."

"And Cathy told you the worst—over the phone?"

"That's right, Steve. Dad's already left Electric Boat. Although Cathy wouldn't say so, I know that he'll never be able to go back. And that means there's no one to support the family—except me. So, you see, I've got to do it. I'm putting in for a hardship discharge soon as we get back to New London. I'm going to try for a job at Electric Boat."

There was nothing Tim could say. He felt as bad as Steve did. He arose, and his hand went to Steve's shoulder.

"That's tough, Steve," Tim said. "What else can I say?"

Steve looked long and hard at his long-time buddy. "You know," he said slowly. "It isn't all bad. Keep this in mind. Somebody's got to build these ships you're going to be traveling on. And I hope to be the one to do it. Nuclear power for all kinds of ships is the coming thing—you wait and see."

[ *177* ]

The boys grinned at one another. Life was going to be all right after all.

"You make 'em and I'll sail 'em," Tim said.

"Aye, aye, Captain Borden of the United States Navy."

# About the Author

ROBERT N. WEBB was born in Dayton, Ohio, but has lived near Boston in recent years. Inspired by the "Cradle of Liberty," he has developed an insatiable interest in American history and history-in-the-making. He has brought to this thrilling tale of the voyage of the *Nautilus* the skill and accuracy of a trained newspaper reporter and editor. The author of several well-regarded adult novels, he now concentrates on writing for children and has, in his own youngsters, Kink and Judy, an admiring though occasionally critical audience.

## About the Illustrator

FRANK VAUGHN comes from New Rochelle, New York, where he went to school and later won two scholarships to the New York Phoenix School of Design. He has done extensive magazine and advertising illustrations as well as art work for numerous children's books. His own personal experiences while in the United States Navy make his illustrations for WE WERE THERE ON THE NAUTILUS very real indeed. Mr. Vaughn now lives with his wife and three children in New City, New York.

## About the Historical Consultant

CAPTAIN WILLIAM R. ANDERSON was born in Bakersville, Tennessee. After graduation from Columbia Military Academy in his home state, he attended the United States Naval Academy at Annapolis, Maryland. When the atomic-powered submarine *Nautilus* crossed the geographic North Pole, it was under the command of young Captain Anderson, who was awarded the Legion of Merit for completing his mission. He has also received a host of awards and citations for the extensive scientific data collected under his leadership during the voyage. With all these achievements to his credit, it is no wonder his wife and two sons think of him as a pretty special Dad.

# WE WERE THERE BOOKS